Once You Love a Scoundrel

Once You Love a Scoundrel

SCANDALOUS GENTLEMEN BOOK THREE

DAWN BROWER

Contents

EXCERPT: WHEN I LOVED A CHARMER

EXCERPT: COURTING A CHRISTMAS WALLFLOWER

For all those that find strength when they need it most. Do not give up. You never know what you might discover in the middle of your journey.

You must be the best judge of your own happiness.

— JANE AUSTEN, EMMA

December 1866

VIOLET FOLLOWED IRIS DOWN THE FORBIDDEN PATH. Iris couldn't believe her always follows the rules sister had suggested they take this scandalous walk. Once Violet had made the proposal, Iris would not allow her to retract it. She had been hoping to inspect the trail one day, and this might be her only chance.

It was a narrow pathway that was covered in snow. There were some footprints leading down the passage. Someone had been this way, but it would be difficult to determine when they had last been there. The snow wasn't too deep, but her skirts would be drenched after their little adventure. She didn't care about that. Elation filled her to her very core.

"This is so exciting," Iris said in a giddy tone. She clapped her hands. "I'm so glad you thought to do this."

"I'm happy you're having such an exhilarating time." Violet replied, but she didn't sound nearly as eager as Iris felt. Well, that was too bad. She would have to see it through, whether or not she liked it.

"How many couples do you think sneak down this path?" Iris picked up the pace and was running down the path now. She could still hear Violet's groan as she moved through the snow.

"Don't go too far," Violet called out.

Iris was past hearing her sister. She disappeared into the trees. It would be so easy to find a place to hide with a gentleman. If she were to come on this path, she would hope the man by her side would be the Earl of Hampstead. He was the handsomest man Iris had ever laid eyes on. His hair was dark and silky looking, but it was those eyes of his that called to her. They were so blue they were near the color of the ice, now dripping down from the tree branches. The blue more of a light tint. Eerie to behold; however, enticing at the same time. She shivered at the very thought of catching the earl's attention.

"Lady Iris," a man called out.

She stopped short. It couldn't be… Why was the Earl of Hampstead walking on Scandal Lane? More importantly, why was he calling her name? Iris spun on her heel and headed in the direction of his voice. She had been thrilled to explore the forbidden path, but now… This was the opportunity she had been hoping for.

"Lord Hampstead," she said breathlessly when she caught up with him. His dark hair was stunning against the backdrop of snow. A patch fell from a nearby branch and landed on his shoulder. She giggled when he scowled and brushed it off. "Why are you here?" she asked.

"I've been sent to retrieve you," he replied in a congenial tone. "Your sister is worried."

Iris frowned. She had told Violet about her plan to trap Lord Hampstead into marriage. He was a rogue, and one of the infamous Scandalous Gentleman. He was unlikely to willingly ask a woman for their hand in marriage. Iris wanted to be his wife, and she would do almost anything to make that dream come true. "My sister sent you?" Skepticism filled her tone as she spoke. Violet had been adamantly against Iris's plan.

"I volunteered," he answered. "Lord Merrifield is keeping Lady Violet company until we can join them."

A sly smile formed on her face. She couldn't help wondering if fate was offering her exactly what she desired. This couldn't have happened better if she had planned it herself. She would be a fool to pass on this fortuitous event. "Do we have to return right away." Iris stepped closer. "My sister fancies herself in love with the marquess. Maybe if they had a few moments alone, they could make a…connection."

It wasn't a total lie. There had been a time when Lord Merrifield had appealed to Violet. Iris wasn't certain when that had changed or why, but she wasn't above using that former infatuation to her advantage. Violet would forgive her for it. Her sister always forgave her.

"She does?" Lord Hampstead lifted a brow, then frowned. "I hadn't been aware of that." He glanced behind him. "I may have made a mistake."

"I'm sure you're wrong." Iris lifted her hand and placed it on his chest. "You don't seem as if you would ever do anything so foolish."

He glanced down at her, meeting her gaze. "I try not to, but it appears as if it is a day for them." He lifted his hand and removed her hand from his chest. "We need to return. Please allow me to escort you back to your sister's side."

Iris frowned. What had she done wrong? "Do you not find me pretty?" Lord Hampstead was a rogue. Didn't all gentlemen of his ilk take advantage of willing females?

"Lady Iris…" He glanced away. "Your beauty or lack thereof isn't an issue here." He stepped away from her.

Cold seeped through her at his words. He didn't think she was pretty. That was what she heard in his tone. She had made an utter fool of herself. "I see," she said. "So, asking you to kiss me isn't something you're interested in either."

She blew out a breath. If she couldn't entice him. Which meant there was no real chance of seducing him and trapping him into marriage. So much for her plan. Violet would be relieved to discover Iris wouldn't be causing a scandal.

"Lady Iris," Lord Hampstead said in a soft tone. "You don't want a man like me. I'm not a good man."

She lifted her head and met his cool gaze with

her own. "Don't presume to know what I want." Her tone was filled with bitterness. "But I do have to know one thing before…" She shook her head. "I just need to know." Iris stomped forward and wrapped her arms around his neck, then pulled herself up so she could press her lips to his.

He didn't move for a moment, but then he returned the kiss. Almost as if he couldn't help himself. It was everything Iris had imagined it could be. Sweet, sensual, and filled with heat that threatened to consume her. But it ended before it could truly become the inferno in threatened to be. Lord Hampstead yanked his head away and pushed her from him. "You shouldn't have done that." He wiped his hand over his mouth as if the touch of her lips to his had been an insult.

"You liked it," she told him. "Don't deny the truth."

"The truth is, little girl, you are not the temptation you believe yourself to be." He stiffened. "I don't have an interest in tutoring the innocent. I prefer a woman that already knows how to please a man."

"You're a bastard," she spat out the words. Pain filled her heart. He had made it very clear she wasn't for him. When he looked at her, he felt no desire. That kiss had meant far more to her than it ever would to him.

"You best remember that." He glared at her, but then held out his arm. "Come, I'll take you back to your sister."

"I don't need your help." She shoved his arm away. "I can find my own way back."

They walked in silence most of the way back. She almost tripped, and he caught her as they exited the trees. "Let go of me," Iris snapped at him. He held up his hands and let her keep walking on her own.

Lady Iris stormed away from Lord Hampstead and stopped by Lady Violet. "Let's go home. This has been the worst day."

"Of course," Violet told her. "It's cold and wet, anyway. We'll have tea by the fire and warm ourselves."

"Yes," Lady Iris said and sniffled. "That sounds wonderful."

Violet led Iris out of the path and the gentleman walked behind them solemnly. After a few moments, Lord Merrifield asked the earl. "What did happen?"

"I don't wish to discuss it," Lord Hampstead replied in a sour tone.

"That good was it?" Zachariah couldn't help teasing him. "She's a pretty chit. Did you try to steal a kiss?"

"I said I don't wish to discuss it," Lord Hampstead said through gritted teeth.

They were not talking as quietly as they thought they were. Iris could hear every word. She wanted to scream at them both to be quiet, but she held her tongue. It had been an embarrassing day, and she never wanted to think about it again.

They finally exited the path, and Iris breathed a sigh of relief. There was no one around to gossip about their adventure. Before she had been so thoroughly rebuked by the earl she would have been glad to have been caught. It would have been a good reason for the earl to propose marriage. Now, though…it was the last thing she wanted.

"Should we follow them until they reach home?" Lord Merrifield asked the earl.

"It is probably a good idea. We can ensure they don't find any more trouble." Lord Hampstead didn't sound any happier than Iris felt.

"Surely you don't think they would decide on

another adventure so soon after the last one." Zachariah said, doubt in his tone.

"With that one it is best to always be on your guard." Hampstead muttered. He was talking about her. Iris stiffened at his words. Despite that, she didn't turn around. She fully intended to pretend he didn't exist.

"Fair enough," Lord Merrifield said in a light tone. He sounded so happy. Why did the marquess have that amused tone? Had something happened between him and Violet? Doubtfully… He was probably entertained by the earl's sour mood. Men could be so contrary.

They walked in silence until they reached their home. Once they were inside, Iris closed her eyes and took a deep breath. All her dreams had been shattered, and nothing would ever be the same again. Suddenly, the idea of her Christmas ball didn't sound as wonderful as it once had. There was no turning back now, though. The invitations had been sent. She would have to see it through, even if her heart was no longer in it. Lord Hampstead had shattered it thoroughly. Iris didn't think she would ever love again.

One year later...

Daniel Andrews, the Earl of Hampstead, leaned back in his chair. Pain had started to pound inside his head. More specifically right behind his eyes. The responsibilities of the Hampstead estate were extensive, but what he hated the most involved the accounting. The ledgers were filled with numbers. All kinds of numbers... Funds going in and out of the estate coffers, the amount of grains needed to feed the animals on the estate, the supplies needed for the kitchen, or even the sheer amount of candles they used on a weekly basis. It never ended. There were too many things to keep track of and not enough hours in the day to go over it all. Overseeing it all had taken up the majority of his time, and he wish he didn't have to undertake so much on his own. He had been born into the title, and while he understood that it was a privilege, he still hated most of it. Sometimes he wished he had been born a second son with less responsibility.

"Daniel," a female said in a soft tone.

Speaking of responsibilities... "Yes, Calliope?" He lifted his gaze to meet hers. His sister stood in front of his desk with her hands behind her back and a pensive expression on her lovely face. Her golden blonde curls pinned on top of her head, but most of it was plaited and twisted into a chignon. Her day dress was a cornflower blue that matched her eyes. He adored his sister, but his head already hurt. He wasn't certain he wanted to add her current dilemma to his already long list of duties.

"About the invitation to the Christmastide..."

"No," he interrupted her. The last thing he wanted was to attend a Christmastide house party. All right, that wasn't true, but it was a close second. It would be a fortnight of socializing and putting on a smile, as if nothing in the world bothered him. "We are not going."

"Please," Calliope said in a pleading tone. "It'll

help me. In a few months I'll have my come out and this will give me a chance to learn some of the social skills I'll need. These are people you socialize with regularly, isn't it? Why don't you want to go?"

Daniel pinched the bridge of his nose. The pain had intensified with each word she spoke. "I hate Christmastide," he reminded her.

She pouted. "Then be grumpy the entire time. It is what you do every year, anyway." Calliope placed her palms on his desk and met his gaze. "I want my season to be successful. Please don't be difficult and help me."

Calliope would be eight and ten in a month, and her first season would be, as she said soon. The Christmastide party was informal, and she had been invited along with him. She was right, of course. It would be beneficial for her. She could become more acquainted with the Duchess of Lindsey, the hostess of the event, and that connection at her back she would be nearly guaranteed a success. Daniel wanted the best for his sister, and that meant he would have to agree to attend the blasted party. "I'll consider it," he told her.

She rolled her eyes. "Consider fast. We will have to depart London soon if we're going to travel to the Duke of Lindsey's home in the country."

"Is that so?" He fought a smile. "I hadn't realized that. If you need an answer now, I believe I already gave you one."

She groaned. "Why are you being so difficult?" She plopped down on a chair near his desk. "I thought you loved me." Her tone was full of the exasperation she projected quite dramatically before him. "Why can't you just say yes?"

"Has anyone ever told you that patience is a virtue?"

She pinned him with a glare so ferocious he nearly winced from the impact. "Has anyone ever told you that your behavior is tedious?"

His lips twitched. "Yes," he replied in an amused tone. "You have. Several times in fact."

"It bears repeating," she said in a droll tone. "Now about the house party?"

Daniel shouldn't have allowed this conversation to continue. He had ledgers to go through and expenditures to approve. Instead, he had decided to tease his sister a little, and the pain in his head continued to beat on. He rubbed his temples, but it didn't help. Nothing seemed to ease the pain. Perhaps he should take a break. "All right," he conceded. He had planned to, but his sister didn't need to know that. "We can go. We will even leave early." The dratted ledgers could wait until they returned. "Lindsey asked me to come before his wife's family descended upon them. Have your maid pack your trunk. We will leave at dawn."

She clapped her hands in excitement. "Have I ever told you that you are my favorite brother."

He narrowed his gaze. "I am your only brother."

"Then it is fortunate that I like you." She stood. "Thank you," she said in an earnest tone. "Christmas isn't your favorite time of the year. I want you to know I do understand that." She smiled. "It sounds as if the duke does too. Is that why he asked you to come early." She tilted her head to the side. "Wait... If you already planned to go, why did you tell me no?"

He shook his head. "I was going to write to Lindsey and decline the invitation. I received his missive earlier today. I haven't had time to respond." His friends did know why he hated Christmas, but he doubted that was why Lindsey asked him to arrive early. "Instead, I'll send it ahead of us so they know to expect our arrival."

"Oh, all right," she said absentmindedly. "Then I'll let you finish your business and I'll have Lucy start packing for me. I'll see you later for the evening meal."

After she left, Daniel blew out a breath. He closed the ledgers and organized his desk. With those tasks done, he left his study and went to his room. He would have to prepare to leave in the morning as well, but he would have to rest. Otherwise, his head pain would never go away...

IRIS STARED OUT OF THE WINDOW IN THE SITTING room. She hated this time of the year. It used to be her favorite, but ever since last year and her little excursion on Scandal Lane, she had grown to dislike it. A lot. The Earl of Hampstead was a large part of that hate. For a few brief moments, she had thought everything would be perfect. The kiss had started out wonderful. Until it had all fallen apart before her eyes. She would never forget that look on his face. As if she were something distasteful, and he had to wipe that foulness from his mouth.

It had hurt so damn much...

He had tried to apologize at the ball. Had even danced with her. It was a waltz that had seemed as if it went on forever. If it had been pleasant, she would have liked that part. Instead, it had been awkward and unbearable. She had to pretend it was enjoyable, though. Her face had hurt from forcing herself to smile through the entire dance. Any conversation they'd had...well, it had been stilted and formal. Luckily, during the season the Earl of Hampstead had been absent. That part hadn't surprised her. The earl didn't attend social events as a rule. The ball she had planned during Christmas-tide was an exception. He had accepted the invita-tion well before the incident on Scandal Lane.

Next season though... His younger sister would have her come out, and then he would attend several social gatherings. He would have to escort her to them. She could not avoid him for much longer, and in that she was dreading the upcoming season. He would probably also be at the Christ-mastide house party her good friend, Francesca, the Duchess of Lindsey, was hosting. As much as Iris would like to attend the party, she would have to decline. If she went, she would be miserable the entire time.

She would spend Christmastide alone. It was for the best.

"Hello," her sister, Violet, said as she entered the sitting room. "I'm glad you're home."

She turned to meet Violet's gaze. "Where else would I be?" Her tone was monotone as she spoke.

Violet waved her hand dismissively. "Oh, I don't know. Paying a call on someone."

"The only ladies I visit are you and Francesca. As Francesca is in the country and you are here, I would think it obvious where you could find me." Her bitterness was a sharp knife, and it couldn't be contained. Even with the sister she adored. Violet was happily married, and sometime Iris didn't think she understood how unhappy she had become. Her sister had a husband that adored her. They had their share of difficulties. The Marquess of Merrifield doted on Violet. Iris was glad for that. She wanted Violet to be happy. The problem was, it made her own unhappiness even more noticeable.

"You're right," Violet agreed, then sighed. "Please accept my apology. I had hoped that if I kept a light tone, it might help..."

"Brighten my dull spirits," Iris finished for her. How could she be so bloody selfish? Her sister was trying to help her and Iris should be better. "I should be the one apologizing. Thank you for visiting." Iris tried to keep her tone jovial, but it came out much less than that. "When do you depart for Lindsey?"

"In the morning," Violet told her. "That is why I am here. I had hoped to change your mind."

"You're leaving so soon?" The house party wasn't supposed to begin for another sennight. "Why?" She ignored the last part of Violet's statement. Iris had no intention of changing her mind about attending.

"Lindsey asked Zachariah to come early." Violet shrugged. "I don't mind. It gives me more time with Francesca before her hostess duties begin."

"That is lovely," Iris said. "How is Francesca?"

"She's doing well," Violet told her. "But you're going to see that for yourself. We will be here in the morning to retrieve you."

They were back to that again... "I told you I am not attending the house party." She didn't know why Violet was being so stubborn about it. "I don't want to go."

"Well," Violet began. "As I stated earlier, I had hoped to change your mind."

"You're not going to," she interrupted her.

"I don't need to," Violet said, then smirked.

Iris narrowed her gaze. She had to have heard her sister incorrectly. "I'm confused." She tilted her head to the side. "If you don't need to convince me to go, why do you seem so thrilled."

"Because father is ordering you to attend." She grinned. "I spoke with him before I came in here to speak to you. He agrees it will be good for you."

"What?" She glared at her sister. How could Violet have done this to her? Lord Hampstead was going to be there. Iris could not see him again. At least not until she was happily married to another man and could pretend nothing had happened between them. "No. Just no."

"It's too late, little sister," Violet told her. "I already told your maid. She is packing your trunk now. It's going to be fun. Quit being so grumpy about Christmastide. It is time for you to remember how much you love this time of the year." With those words, Violet stood. "I know why you won't go, but you shouldn't let him prevent you from doing something that will make you happy. Take back what it is important despite him." She placed a hand on her sister's shoulder. "You deserve happiness."

She didn't give Iris a chance to say anything else. Iris wanted to stay mad, but she couldn't find the motivation to continue sulking. Instead, she resigned herself to her fate. She had no choice. The Christmastide party would be in her future, and Violet was right. She *did* deserve to be happy.

The journey to the Duke of Lindsey's country estate took them three days. Three cold, mind-numbing days... Daniel had almost enjoyed that part. It was far preferable to the head pain that he'd had to endure while going over the estate ledgers. The rest of the trip had not been as enjoyable. Calliope hated traveling, and the frigid temperature didn't help her demeanor.

So, when they finally arrived at the Lindsey estate, Daniel had breathed a sigh of relief. He couldn't wait to step out of the carriage and stretch his legs. When the carriage rolled to a stop at the entrance, Daniel did just that. He only halted long enough to assist his sister out of the carriage. Then he stomped up the front steps and banged on the door.

"So kind of you to wait for me to walk with you," Calliope said as she caught up with him. "You're quite the gentleman, brother."

Daniel met her gaze and grinned. "Thank you," he replied in an amused tone. "I've always prided myself on being a gentleman."

Calliope rolled her eyes. "I would think most ladies consider you a scoundrel."

"Thank you," he agreed, then winked.

At that moment, the door opened. An elderly man with snow white hair and faded brown eyes stood in the entrance. "Yes?"

"I am Lord Hampstead, and this is Lady Calliope Andrews. Their Graces are expecting us."

"Indeed," the elderly man said. "Please come in. I'll have the footman see to your trunks."

Calliope and Daniel strolled inside. While still in the foyer, they removed their cloaks and handed them to the butler. After a few moments, the Duke of Lindsey strolled in. "Hampstead," Lindsey said, in a jovial tone. "You're the first to arrive. I was just going to look for my wife. I trust your journey went well."

"Aside from the cold," he said. "And Calliope's

constant petulant complaints. Indeed, it was most pleasant."

His sister rolled her eyes. "Don't listen to him, Your Grace." She smiled. "He's terrible to travel with." She glared at Daniel. "We're both happy to be here. Thank you for the invitation."

The duke's lips twitched. "I'm familiar with Hampstead's dislike of travel. I understand it is a familial trait as well." His eyes gleamed with amusement. "I'm glad you were both brave enough to endure it and join us. Please follow me to the sitting room. The duchess should be there with afternoon tea. Unless you would prefer to be shown to your rooms so you can rest."

"I'd prefer tea," Calliope said. "I can rest later."

Daniel wasn't at all surprised by his sister's choice. She was probably still a little cold and wanted tea to help warm her. He would prefer a stronger beverage than tea. "I don't suppose you have brandy instead?"

Lindsey shook his head. "No, at least not in the sitting room. We can retire to my study later for a snifter or two."

"All right," Daniel agreed.

Before they could depart, another bang on the door caught their attention. The butler was nowhere to be found. Lindsey cursed and went to answer his own door. Daniel was amused to see a duke doing what he normally had servants for. Lindsey opened the door and grinned. "Goodland," he said in a cheery tone. "I thought you were coming later." He gestured for the viscount to come inside.

Goodland stepped into the foyer and unbuttoned his coat. "I wrapped up my business early and thought, why the hell not come earlier. It won't be too much trouble, will it?"

Lindsey shook his head. "No, your chamber should already be prepared. The servants have been preparing for this house party for days now."

"Wonderful," Goodland replied, and shrugged out of his coat. The butler returned at that moment and took it from the viscount.

"I'll take that, my lord," the butler said, then left.

Goodland turned toward Daniel and Calliope. "Hampstead," he shouted in a jovial tone. "I saw your carriage being taken to the stable. There is a stack of trunks out there to be brought inside. Did you bring your entire wardrobe with you?"

Daniel glared at him. "Only one of those trunks belongs to me."

"I'm afraid the rest are mine," Calliope said. Her cheeks pinkened as she met Goodland's gaze. "Gowns take up a lot of space."

Was Calliope embarrassed because she had so many trunks. Daniel narrowed his gaze. "You don't need to explain yourself to the viscount. He likes to tease. Ignore him. The rest of us do."

"He is right," Goodland agreed. "They do ignore me. Even when they shouldn't." He winked. "I hope you do not follow his lead." He held a hand over his chest. "It would break what's left of my poor abused heart."

"Do not listen to that nonsense," Daniel ordered Calliope. He turned to Goodland. "And you stay away from my sister."

The last thing he needed was for Calliope to fall for Goodland. The only broken heart would be hers. The only gentleman more determined to never marry than Daniel, was Goodland. The viscount had his reasons for remaining unwed, and Daniel didn't blame him for his reluctance. That didn't mean he would allow him to ruin his sister. Calliope would find a man worthy of her. One that would not only treat her with respect but would always put her needs first. Goodland was not the man to do that for her. He was incapable of it.

"Hampstead, you're being exceedingly tedious today."

Daniel almost stepped forward. To do what he wasn't certain. One look from Lindsey and he refrained. "I think we should go for that tea now."

"Excellent idea," Lindsey said. "Follow me."

The duke led them down a corridor in his sprawling castle until they finally arrived at the sitting room. The duchess was indeed inside, and tea was sitting on a nearby cart. They all settled in for afternoon tea. The conversation stilted, and there was no sign that it would improve either.

IRIS STARED OUT THE WINDOW OF THE CARRIAGE. They were getting close to the ducal estate. As the distance closed between them and the castle, Iris's anxiety grew. She couldn't be certain if the Earl of Hampstead was there yet or not, but that didn't matter. He would be there eventually if he wasn't already, and that was all that mattered. Then she would be forced to speak to him. At least it wouldn't be all the time. She could ignore him for the most part, and she would. But there were still social niceties she would have to observe. That was what she wished she could avoid.

"There it is," Violet said, excitement in her tone. "It's massive."

"The joys of being a duke," Violet's husband, the Marquess of Merrifield, said.

Violet wrinkled her nose. "You'll be a duke some-day, and the Merrifield estate is quite large. Don't act as if you don't have something comparable."

"That is true," the marquess agreed. "But at least I'm not the one responsible for this gathering. That means I can relax and enjoy Lindsey's discom-fort." The marquess grinned. "And that will be as massive as his estate."

"Don't you think that is unkind?" Iris asked. She couldn't fathom why he would wish his friend discomfort. "Isn't he your friend?"

"No," Lord Merrifield replied. "It is not callous. Because we are friends, we can tease him. It'll help him suffer through it all."

Violet frowned. "I don't think I will ever under-stand your friendship."

"It's best not to think about it too much. Chances are you will develop a head pain from it." Lord Merrifield shrugged. "We quit trying to dissect our friendship when we were still boys. It works, and that is all that matters to us."

Iris almost envied them. The five of them had been dubbed the Scandalous Gentleman. Three of them were married now. The only two left unattached were the Earl of Hampstead and the Viscount of Goodland. Many ladies had hopes of catching their attention, especially now that three had fallen in love and were happily married.

At one time, Iris had hoped to be the one Hampstead would love. Now she just wanted to pretend she had never been so bloody foolish. Fate wasn't allowing her that privilege, though. She would have to face her mistake, or she would never be able to move forward. That was what she had decided to do during this house party. Set aside her past and look to her future. One that would never include a scoundrel like the Earl of Hampstead.

"That seems like sound advice," Iris said to Lord Merrifield. She turned to Violet. "I would heed what your husband has suggested. Besides, it involves his friends. You don't need to understand it, do you?"

"I suppose you're right," Violet told her. "As long as he loves me, I don't care who his friends are.

If Lord Hampstead and Lord Goodland find wives, it will all sort itself out."

"I wouldn't hold your breath," Lord Merrifield said. "Those two are unlikely to marry, and both have reasons for that decision. They're confirmed bachelors."

Iris frowned. "Didn't all of you say that once upon a time?"

Violet's eyes widened. "You're not still hoping..." Concern was etched into her sister's eyes as she met Iris's gaze. Iris barely held back a groan. She would have to ensure her sister she had no desire to trap the Earl of Hampstead into marriage.

"I'm not," Iris interrupted Violet. She didn't need her sister to put into words what she had once foolishly desired. "Reforming a scoundrel is the last thing I wish to do." She shrugged. "I had thought though, that since all of them had believed they would never marry, how can your husband be certain the final two won't."

"Our reasons were not the same as theirs." Lord Merrifield frowned. "I can't tell you their secrets, but rest assured, they are profound. If they marry, I will be shocked to the core. Winchester, Lindsey, and I...we just enjoyed our freedom. Until we realized that there can be more to marriage if we opened our heart to it. Goodland and Hampstead...their hearts were shattered a long time ago. They have nothing left to offer a woman."

Iris frowned. She wondered what had happened to them. Lord Merrifield seemed so certain that neither one would marry. Should she feel sorry for them? Perhaps, and a part of her did; however, that did not mean that her own demons hadn't been excised. "That's unfortunate for them," she said softly. "It means they'll never know true happiness." Some days she didn't think she would either.

"That is the fate some must face," Lord Merrifield told her. "I'm fortunate, and thankful for it each day. If I could change things for them, I would. It would be wonderful if all my friends found the same happiness I have."

"Yes," Violet agreed. She met Iris's gaze. "It's what I want for you too." Her tone was filled with so much warmth and love. Iris was grateful she had such a wonderful twin sister. She and Violet had always been close, and she had missed having her in the house.

"There is still hope for me," Iris told her sister. "My heart hasn't been destroyed. The right man will come into my life, and then the possibilities will be endless." First she had to expunge a certain earl from her heart for good. If she still thought about him, that meant he still had a hold on her. It was past time she let go.

Violet smiled. "I hope so." Concern was etched through her voice as she spoke. Iris couldn't dwell on that. She had to remain focused. Violet had her husband to lean on, and she had to stop worrying so much about Iris. Somehow, she would make her sister see that.

With those words, the carriage came to a stop in front of the Lindsey estate. Lord Merrifield stepped out of the carriage and assisted Iris and Violet out. They all walked to the front door as the footman saw to their trunks. The Christmastide house party had begun. For Iris, it was the beginning of the future she hoped to seize. Tomorrow would bring her happiness. She would make sure of it, even if she had to reshape the longing inside her heart and every single one of her expectations to accept it.

Iris wanted to hide in her bedchamber, but also realized she couldn't do any such thing. Her sister had demanded she socialize with everyone that attended the house party. Most of them would not arrive for a few more days, but there were guests already in the house. Which meant Iris would have to stop hiding and pretend she was happy to be attending the Christmastide celebration.

She sighed and then exited her bedchamber. Francesca planned to have afternoon tea in her favorite sitting room of the castle. They had arrived too late to join them the day before for tea, but Iris could go spend some time with her friends now. She adored Francesca, and Adeline was due to arrive soon. It also helped that Violet was there. In truth, there wasn't much reason for her to avoid tea time. It was unlikely that the one person she wished to avoid would join them. The ladies would be left alone, at least this early on. Once everyone arrived, there would be guests all over the house doing a variety of activities.

Iris could not escape so easily then...

Her footsteps echoed through the corridor as she made her way to the sitting room. When she reached her destination, she pushed open the door. The tea service had not yet arrived, but her friends had. Francesca, Violet, and a woman Iris hadn't met sat inside the room.

"Iris," Francesca called out to her. "Come sit," she patted the cushion on the settee next to her. "We've been waiting for you."

Iris did as the duchess asked and sat next to her. "Have I missed anything?" She didn't know what they could possibly be discussing. It seemed like a reasonable question.

"Not much," the lady she hadn't recognized said. "I was complaining about my overprotective brother."

"Oh?" Iris didn't have a brother, so she didn't know what that was like. "Who is your brother?"

"The Earl of Hampstead." The lady wrinkled her nose. "He's being his usually tedious self."

Iris froze and stared at the young woman. This was the earl's little sister. She had been aware he had a sister, but she never expected her to be in attendance. Iris did her best to remain calm. It was his sister, not him. She could handle this. "What is he doing that is so atrocious?" At least the earl was unlikely to openly snub his own sister.

"To quote him," the lady began. "Calliope, you're to stay away from Lord Goodland. He's not for you."

Before anyone could respond, a maid brought in the tea cart. Francesca dealt with the maid, then poured everyone tea. Once they all had cups in hand, they returned to the conversation. It was Violet that responded to Lady Calliope's remarks. "He is being protective," Violet told her. "But he has a good reason for it. If anyone knows the viscount, it is your brother. You should heed his advice."

Lady Calliope sighed. "It's not as if I set my cap for him." She took a sip of her tea. "I was being polite, nothing more. I won't officially have my come out until spring." She shrugged. "I don't plan on settling down with the first man that I cross paths with. I plan on enjoying my season."

Iris had to smile at that. "As well you should." She decided in that moment she liked Lady Calliope. "And don't let your brother prevent you from doing so either." She hoped Lady Calliope gave her brother a troublesome time as much as possible. It was a bit mean of her to wish it on him, but she never claimed to be a nice person.

"It has always been a goal of mine to drive him mad," Lady Calliope admitted. "He's too serious most of the time." She set her tea down. "Especially this time of the year. It would do him good to find something to smile about. I wish he would consider marriage himself, but he's so..." She shook her head. "I've said too much."

In Iris's opinion, she hadn't said enough. She was insanely curious. What was it about Christmastide that made Lord Hampstead especially grumpy? She was about to ask when the door opened and Adeline, the Countess of Winchester, walked in. "Oh, good," she began. "I didn't miss tea."

Her blonde curls were pinned elegantly on top of her head, and her cheeks were tinged pink. Probably from the cold. Francesca stood and hugged her cousin. "I'm so glad you're here."

"Not as much as I am," Adeline replied. "My husband has already gone off in search of yours."

"They're playing billiards, I believe," Violet said. "And probably complaining about something."

"My brother is probably doing that the most." Lady Calliope picked up her tea. "But I have noticed they're all doing it a lot. Why?"

"Because they're men," Francesca said. "Not one of them planned on marriage, but here we all are." She frowned. "Well, three of us anyway."

"And we all know they're happily married," Violet began. "Even if it didn't start that way. I think this is all masculine pride. As if admitting how happy they are is somehow wrong." She shrugged. "I gave up trying to decipher their motivation."

Francesca handed Adeline a cup of tea. "It's best not to try," she agreed. "Let them have their bonding and brandy."

Iris sat back quietly and listened to them. Was this what marriage was like? They all seemed happy, and their talk didn't distract from that. They were all right with their husbands' behavior, as if they had some secret they couldn't share with the rest, or perhaps they didn't need to share it. Because it was understood between them all. The married ladies could just look at each other and some silent communication passed between them.

It didn't sit well with her. She felt as if suddenly she didn't belong anymore. These women were her closest friends, and she had always been able to count on them. Now, though, she felt incredibly alone. As if she lost something she might never have again. She set down her tea and stood. Her stomach roiled, and she had to leave. "Please excuse me," she forced the words out. "I don't feel well. I'm going to my chamber to rest."

She didn't give them time to respond. Iris rushed out of the room and went directly to her bedchamber. Once there, hot tears fell down her cheeks. Pain filled her, but nothing would ease it. She laid down on her bed and remained there, crying for a long time. Then she sat up, washed her face, and set her feelings aside. There wasn't time for tears anymore. It was time to let her anger go and be a better person, or at least a stronger one.

DANIEL WANTED TO BE BY HIMSELF, BUT HIS FRIENDS would never allow it. They all knew him too well. That was why they had all gathered in the game room for Billiards, and cards. Merrifield avoided cards after he lost a bet a little over a year ago. Even if it had led him to his wife. He claimed he didn't want to chance another moment of bad luck. So he was playing billiards with Goodland.

"Where's the brandy?" the Earl of Winchester said as he entered the room. "It's bloody cold outside. I hate winter."

"Who doesn't?" Goodland asked. "The decanter is over here." He gestured to the bar behind him.

Winchester wandered over to the brandy and poured himself a snifter, then downed the contents. "That's a nice burn," he said, then poured more. "Why is no one else playing?" He nodded toward the billiard table.

"Goodland and Merrifield are being selfish and not allowing us near the table," Lindsey drawled. "Want to play some Faro or Whist? One of you would have to give up billiards to play that though."

"I would not play Faro," Merrifield supplied. "Especially with Hampstead."

"You're only saying that because you lost once," Daniel said, then laughed, but he didn't feel particularly jovial. "Perhaps Winchester has more skill than you."

Daniel didn't want to play cards. It didn't matter what game they chose, but he would. They expected him to. The loneliness in his soul was drowning him from the inside out. For that reason alone, they wouldn't let him be. They knew. This was the time of year he grieved the most, the hardest, for his parents.

They died during Christmastide.

It wasn't just their death, but how they died that haunted him. He could never shake those images from his head, and part of him didn't want to. It was a stark reminder of why he was alone and always would be alone. There was a darkness inside of him that would never leave. Daniel didn't want to subject that darkness on another person. That was why he would remain unmarried.

"We're not done with this game," Merrifield said. "You'll have to go without a fourth for Whist."

"Faro it is," Winchester replied. "Come over here and sit." He gestured toward Daniel and Lindsey. "But no betting. My wife might strangle me if I lose and have to do something foolish."

Lindsey chuckled. "As your wife is related to mine," he began. The two women were cousins. "I suspect she would also be so inclined."

Daniel sighed. "The two of you are not much

fun to play cards with anymore." He grinned. "It is probably wise of you not to make a wager. Especially since I tend to win."

His heart wasn't in the game. Still, he played with skill and his luck held. In this, he had never been required to think too much. Card games came naturally to him, and he'd always been fortunate. If only the rest of his life were like that. It would have made everything much easier. Since he couldn't change any of that, he shoved those thoughts away. "I win again."

"You have the devil's own luck," Winchester said.

Merrifield snorted. "Which is why wagering against him is always a bad idea."

"Too bad you didn't listen to those instincts a year ago," Goodland goaded him. "Much like this billiard game." He smirked. "You lost here too."

This time Daniel did laugh. The expression on Merrifield's face when he realized he had lost was comical. "Games are not for you. Please tell me you didn't make a wager."

Slowly, Merrifield set down his stick, then shook his head. "I didn't. Thankfully," he said, then sighed. "I learned that lesson the hard way. Though it ended up being the best thing that happened to me."

Daniel envied his friends. Three of them had miraculously found the love of their lives. Goodland would unlikely marry. His past had a darkness in it too. That was why he had warned Calliope to stay away from him. His baby sister had a kind heart, and she didn't need Goodland to break it. Much like Daniel had broken Lady Iris Keene's a year ago.

He hadn't meant to do it. That kiss... It had undone him. For a few brief moments, he had let himself become lost in it, in her. Until he remembered why beautiful innocent ladies were not for him. He had to crush his desire for her before it engulfed them both. Lady Iris might hate him now, but what she didn't realize he had done it to save her. From him. She deserved a man much better than him, and one day he would have to see her with that better man. When that happened, it would take every ounce of his strength to keep his distance. Because if there was one woman that tempted him, it was Lady Iris Keene.

He wanted her, and he knew he shouldn't.

Daniel pushed back his chair. "I'm going to

retire in my bedchamber for a little while." He stood. "I'll see you all later."

With those words, he left his friends alone and retired to his bedchamber. Sadness filled him as he walked toward the room. He wasn't fit for polite company. He settled into his bedchamber to rest, but visions of a woman he couldn't have haunted his dreams...

Daniel rolled over and frowned. He hadn't meant to sleep as long as he had. When he had laid down, it hadn't yet been dark in the sky, and now it was pitch black outside. He swung his legs over the side of the bed, then sat up. Clearly he had slept, and soundly, but he felt as if he hadn't truly rested. His dreams had been so vivid.

All of them had been about Lady Iris Keene. Her on a warm sunny day, then dancing in the rain, that day he broke her heart surrounded by snow, and then a final one. That one he couldn't quite shake. She had been warm and naked in his bed with the smile of a well satiated woman. The temptation that image left behind was not something he would be able to shake off easily. Hell, the lady herself had a grip on him. If she had any idea how much he wanted her, he feared she would have used it to her advantage. He wanted her and for that reason alone; he kept his distance.

But damn it was hard...

He sighed. His stomach grumbled, reminding him that he had slept through the evening meal. He hated going into the kitchens when the staff was asleep, but he would have to find something to eat. If he had to wake a servant, he would feel like an arse. At least he had the good sense to remove his waistcoat, jacket, and boots before laying down. His shirt was wrinkled, but it would have to do. The collar was open and loose, but that wouldn't matter either. No one would see him. At least he hoped no one would.

Daniel slipped his feet into his boots, then exited the bedchamber. The kitchen would be his first stop, then he would settle into the library. He didn't bother with a candle. His eyes had adjusted to the dark, and he visited often enough that he knew his way around the castle. If he could navigate it while inebriated, he shouldn't have too much trouble now.

He reached the kitchen and fumbled around in

the dark until he found something for a meal. He took a small chunk of cheese and the end piece of a loaf of bread. It would do to settle his stomach. When he reached the library, he could help himself to Lindsey's brandy. Daniel munched on the bread and cheese as he wandered down the hall. When he reached the library, he was surprise to discover some candles were lit along with a fire in the hearth.

"Well that is convenient," he mumbled to himself. A servant must have forgotten to take care of the candles and the fire. He would do it before he left the room.

Daniel went straight to the brandy and poured a snifter. He drank the contents in one gulp to wash down the cheese and bread, then poured more to savor. Perhaps he would find a book to read. What else did he have to do at this time of night. He blew out a breath and turned to go look at the shelves. He froze when he realized the room was not empty, as he had assumed.

A lady with golden blonde hair knelt before a book shelf studying the tomes on the bottom shelf. She nibbled on her lip and pushed a stray lock of hair behind her ear. How had she not heard him come in? Daniel took a moment to just look at her. Once she realized she wasn't alone, her entire demeanor would change, and she wouldn't look upon him fondly.

He should leave before she noticed him. It would be for the best. Especially considering his earlier dreams about her. They were still there inside his mind, leaving his skin hot and his cock so hard it bordered on pain. He closed his eyes and reminded himself to breathe. There wasn't enough brandy in the library to help him through this upcoming ordeal. It would be best to fumble through it now in private, then in front of the other guests. He cleared his throat, "Pardon me..."

She moved her head in a fast, jerky motion and when her gaze landed on his... He sucked in a breath and held it. Those blue eyes were as stunning as he remembered. It was like a punch to the gut. His dreams hadn't done her justice. "What are you doing in here?" she asked. Her tone was filled with irritation.

It was then he realized what she was wearing... He had been so focused on that lovely face that he hadn't looked beyond that. She had on a wrapper over her shift, and if that shift fell... God, help him. It would be so easy to strip her bare and kiss every inch of her creamy skin. His temptation and his damnation all in one. He lifted a brow. "I could ask you the same thing. Shouldn't you be hiding in your bedchamber?"

Please go back to your bedchamber...

He quietly begged her to run away from him before he did something foolish. He was so close to the edge, and he couldn't find one reason not to step over and lose himself in his desire. There were many reasons for him not to touch her, and somehow he had to remember every single one of them. The biggest one, though, was her. She didn't need him to touch her, and she definitely hadn't invited him to.

She glared at him. "I haven't been hiding," she seethed. "It's only been one day." Lady Iris stood and folded her arms over her chest. The action plumped those pert breasts of hers up and his gaze flew to them. He was a man and damn it, how could he not look? Besides, I'm not the one that skipped dinner. Perhaps you are the one that has been hiding?" She took a step forward. "Are you afraid of me, my lord?"

WHAT THE HELL WAS WRONG WITH HER? SHE should not be goading the earl. It would not help her, and it definitely would not make the man back away. He had a look in his eyes that gave her pause. The way he stared at her...as if he were a starving man and only she could satiate him. It did funny things to her belly, and heat pooled through her entire body.

And his appearance... Iris wanted to fan herself desperately. She had never seen a man so undressed before. His shirt sleeves were rolled up past the elbow, and with his collar opened up. There was so much skin and temptation. God help her, but she wanted him. This desire going through her was more than she could bear.

He took a sip of his brandy, but his gaze didn't leave hers. "I'm not afraid of you," he said in a husky tone. "You don't have that kind of hold on me."

Of course she didn't... She meant nothing to this man. This scoundrel who took what he wanted without a care of the damage he caused. Damn her foolish heart for falling for him in the first place. Iris had thought she was finally moving past that infatuation. "Then it shouldn't matter that I am in the library looking for something to read." She turned her back to him, but she had a feeling his gaze hadn't wandered away from her. There was too much intensity in his eyes for her to believe otherwise.

"Perhaps you can help me choose something to read," he told her. "I find I am having trouble sleeping."

"Not used to sleeping alone," she shot back. Someone needed to get her out of the room. Iris was having a hard time holding her tongue.

"Are you offering to keep me company?" The sensuality in his voice as he spoke sent shivers down her spine.

She whipped her head around to meet his gaze. There was definitely desire there. She wasn't imagining it, and part of her wanted to step toward him and beg him to kiss her. Iris had too much pride to give into that temptation. "No," she said in a harsh tone. "I deserve far better than what you have to offer." She shrugged and glanced away from him so he couldn't see the hurt his words had brought forward. "My worth is more than that and I won't be a convenient warm body for you to use and forget about."

"I would never forget you," he told her.

Iris would like to believe that, but she knew better. He had made it clear a year ago what he thought about her. She yanked a book off the shelf. She had to exit this library and end this farce of a conversation. Her pride had been stung once, and a repeat of that would not be necessary. "Careful, my lord," she said in an acerbic tone. "Your desperation is showing."

His lips twitched. "I am quite despondent," he agreed. "The prettiest lady in the castle is being a shrew."

She rolled her eyes. Iris placed her hand over her chest and batted her eyelashes. "You think I'm pretty?"

He blinked several times. His gaze focused on her hand, or probably more accurately, her chest. Her wrapper had come undone when she stood up. Her shift wasn't the thickest of garments, and she feared he might be able to see more of her than she wanted him to. "Absolutely stunning," he said in a hoarse tone. "Breathtaking..."

Iris swallowed hard. No, no, no... She didn't need him to desire her. If only he had looked at her this way a year ago. Before he broke her heart... "Stop," she said in a harsh tone.

"I wish I could." The tone in his voice was filled with so much need. "I keep telling myself to walk away, but I can't. I just can't." He stepped toward her and pressed his palm to her cheek. "You're so lovely it hurts to look at you." Lord Hampstead set the snifter on a shelf and then trailed his fingers through her hair.

What was happening? She should step back before anything else happened. Her heart beat heavily inside her chest and she was having trouble breathing. This was all too much. "Lord Hamp-stead..." She could barely utter his name.

"Daniel," he told her. "My name is Daniel. Say it."

Iris shook her head. "I..." She took a deep breath. "I can't do that."

"Yes," he said. "Iris. Say my name."

She didn't. If she did, she would not be able to walk away from him. It didn't matter that he wanted her to say it. Hell, she wanted to say it. But she knew, just knew, that once she did, there was no turning back. "Why are you doing this?"

"Because I'm weak," he said. "And I need you." He didn't give her a chance to say anything else. He lowered his head and pressed his lips to hers. That kiss a year ago didn't compare to this one. It was all raw hunger and desire. He kissed her as if he were dying and this kiss was the only thing that could save him, and she fell into it with a wild abandon.

She should have run out of the room to prevent this from happening.

Because now she knew the truth. His desire could not be feigned. She didn't know the reasons he had pushed her away before, but she wouldn't let him do it again. This kiss stole everything and she couldn't fight it if she wanted to. But she couldn't let it go any farther. Not now. He would not be happy he had given in and kissed her. If Iris had any chance of winning him, she had to fight him. Starting with this kiss.

She pushed back and stepped away from him. Iris met his gaze and wiped her mouth. "Don't do that again." She clutched the book to her chest and walked out of the room. It hurt to do it, but he had to realize he couldn't take what he wanted without a thought to the consequences. She had a fortnight, and she would use it to make him fall in love with her. He had to fight for her or she would never believe he did.

Iris woke from a fitful sleep. Once she had returned to her bedchamber, she had not been able to read. It didn't help that the book she randomly grabbed was a treatise on the best farming techniques. Dry and boring didn't accurately describe how horrid it had been to even skim over. It definitely wasn't something she would have chosen if she had bothered to look at the tome before slipping it off the shelf, then running with it in her hand after Lord Hampstead—Daniel, had kissed her.

She brought her fingers up to her lips. If she concentrated, she could almost feel his lips touching hers again. Iris felt...branded. As if his kiss was permanently etched on her lips and if any other man dared to do the same, she would not enjoy it. What was she going to do? He had made it clear a year ago that he didn't want her. Why would he kiss her now?

His excuse that he was weak was just that, an excuse. Iris didn't believe him. If he had wanted to control himself, he would have. She was not the alluring temptation that he made her out to be. Iris was far from a seductress, and she certainly didn't have the skills one would need to be that enticing.

She snorted. Perhaps she should practice her come-hither looks on him and see what happened. What exactly was a come-hither look? Iris laughed and got out of bed. She stared at herself in the looking glass and frowned. No, she didn't look any different. After a few moments of attempting to look seductive, she gave up. It was a useless endeavor. She didn't have that type of appeal.

Iris rang the bell on her bedside. She would need her maid to help her dress for the day. Mary had been both her and Violet's maid before her sister had married. Mary had opted to stay with her, and Violet found a new maid. One that understood Violet's new station as a marchioness. If Iris ever married, Mary would go with her instead.

Mary strolled into the room. "Good morning,"

she greeted her. "How are you feeling this morning?"

Iris had rested after tea, but had managed to attend the evening meal. Though she had only picked at her food. She had no appetite, but now her stomach grumbled in protest. "I'm famished," she admitted wryly. "Help me dress so I can go down to breakfast."

Her maid smiled. "It's good you have your appetite back. You cannot afford to lose any weight. We wouldn't want you to wither away to nothing."

"I doubt that is likely to happen." She wasn't frail to begin with. Iris had nice curves and a narrow waist. Her bosom wasn't large, but she thought it was all right. Daniel's eyes had traveled over it, at least. He seemed to like it...

She shook that thought away. Iris would not dwell on thoughts of the earl. The scoundrel would only take advantage of her weakness. She would go down to breakfast, and if he was there, she would ignore him. That man did not deserve her attention. Even if she wanted to beg him to kiss her again.

"As long as you eat it, won't," Mary agreed. "Sit so we can fix your hair." She studied Iris's blonde locks. "What did you do to it last night? It's a mess."

Iris sat at the vanity, then shrugged. "I cannot say for certain. The bed didn't like me much last night."

Mary frowned and started to unravel the tangled strands of Iris's hair. It didn't take long for Mary to smooth her locks out and then pin them on top of her head in a chignon. Some curls were left loose to frame her face. "There," Mary said. "Now that is done, what gown would you like to wear today?"

Iris took the time to consider Mary's question. She couldn't recall all the gowns that her maid had packed in Violet's order. Since she hadn't been given a choice to attend this house party and therefore hadn't taken part in planning for it. However, she had noticed the gowns that Mary had unpacked and removed the wrinkled from after they had arrived. "Perhaps the gold one?"

"The one with the lace trim around the bodice and the long sleeves?" Mary asked.

"Yes," Iris confirmed. It was a pretty gown, and she hadn't worn it yet. It seemed like a good day to wear it. Perhaps a certain earl would find it appealing, too. She hated he came to mind first, always in her mind. Nothing seemed to erase him from her thoughts, though.

Mary nodded. "I'll retrieve it, but first let's get your stays tied."

Iris held on to the bedpost as Mary pulled the strings on her stays. Once they were as tight as they would go, Mary tied them in place. After that, it went much smoother finishing her morning routine. "You're lovely," Mary said. "One day a fine gentleman will steal your heart and you'll start down the path your life is meant to take."

"And if I never marry?" She lifted a brow. "Can I not find happiness without a man?"

"Perhaps," Mary conceded. "If we lived in a different time or place, such a thing would be possible. Our lives are tied to the dictates of men."

"And how sad is that…" Iris couldn't argue with her maid's assertion. She had to first live under her father's thumb, and after that, her husband's. Because she was female, she had no actual choices. Some were given to her under the guise of giving her options, but they weren't anything real. If she was lucky enough, she'd marry a man that trusted her enough to make her own decisions. That was something quite rare, though. Violet had a good marriage, and so did Francesca, but she couldn't help wondering how much freedom their husbands allowed them.

"I suppose it is time for me to go down to breakfast," Iris said. Her appetite was dwindling now that she started to think about the future. "Thank you, Mary."

"Enjoy your day, Lady Iris," she said. "Ring for me if you need anything. I'll see to straightening your bedchamber now."

Iris nodded and then left the room. She made her way down the stairs and turned down the hallway that would lead to the breakfast room. Part of her hoped Daniel would be there, and the other part of her hoped he was still sleeping or otherwise occupied. Her heart was so perverse. It both wanted to see him and not see him at the same time.

His cruel words had left her with a shattered heart that had been scattered in the snow like broken shards of glass. Too fine and sharp to pick up and put back together. Now he acted as if he wanted her. Like breathing without her was too difficult. As if she alone could prevent him from gasping his last breath. It was too much. The emotions inside of her had to pick a side. She either wanted him, or she didn't. Otherwise, she wouldn't survive with what was left of her broken heart by the end of this house party.

She reached the door to the breakfast room and

froze. Daniel stood outside of the room, about to open up the door. He glanced up at her and just stared. He seemed as unable to move as her. What were they going to do now?

"Lady Iris," Daniel said in greeting. "I trust you're well this morning."

She kept staring at him as if he were a bug she wanted to crush under her boot. Daniel couldn't blame her. He should not have kissed her in the library. He had lost all sense and given in to the need crawling through him. Somehow, he would have to make things right with her, but he did not know how to even begin doing that.

"I'm perfectly all right," she said in a prim tone. "Are you going to open the door?" She gestured toward where his hand was curved around the handle.

He glanced down and frowned. "Yes," he said. "Are you?"

"If you'll allow me to enter." Her tone was filled with exasperation.

Daniel sighed. She would not make this easy, and he didn't blame her. He had been a right arse the previous night. The ton called him a scoundrel, and he had earned that reputation in his misspent youth, but he hadn't been that wayward man for a couple of years now. He still had lovers, but he was far more discriminate in his choices. What he had never done was accost an innocent lady with unwanted attention. He had never felt more terrible than he did in this moment. He turned the handle and opened the door. "After you," he told her.

She didn't meet his gaze as she slid past him and went inside. They were not alone in the room. He wasn't certain if he was happy about that or not. He should apologize to her, but he also didn't want to call any attention to their time alone in the library. Daniel would not ruin her reputation because he had kissed her without her permission. Lady Winchester sat next to the Duchess of Lindsey. They were family and deep in conversation about the rest of their relatives expected to arrive.

"Iris," the duchess said in greeting. "How are you feeling today?"

"Much better," she answered.

Daniel frowned. She hadn't been feeling well? That was another thing he had to add to his long list of transgressions. Lady Iris went to the buffet set up on one side of the room and filled it with eggs, kippers, and ham. After she had her plate filled, she sat down at the table. A servant brought her a cup of tea, silverware, and a plate with toast. "Will you require anything else, my lady?" the servant inquired.

"No," she said, then smiled at him. "This is fine, thank you."

She was so polite. Daniel clenched his jaw. She wouldn't be that friendly with him. He hated that he hurt her and he wished he could turn back time and change it. There was so much wasted time and sleepless nights over the past year. He had been thinking a lot about what he wanted in his life. All his younger declarations of never marrying or falling in love... Total rubbish.

He didn't want to look back in a couple decades and realize that he let the best thing that he'd ever had slip through his fingers. He wanted her, and damn it, he would find a way to win her. She had been interested in him before. Somehow, he would have to reach that part of her heart again. He didn't want to waste another day. If he had to choose between her and living with his demons, there was no contest. She won every time.

Daniel filled his plate and then sat at the table across from her. He wanted to sit next to her, but it wasn't time for that much closeness. He would have to charm her and she didn't seem inclined to even notice him. "Your Grace," he greeted the duchess. "Lady Winchester." Daniel nodded at them. "How are you this morning?" He didn't glance at Lady Iris, but he could almost feel her glare.

"Please don't be formal with me," the duchess said. "You're one of Matthew's closest friends. Call me Francesca."

"I'm not sure that is wise," he drawled. "Your husband is a jealous man. I like my head where it is."

The duchess laughed. "You don't have any plans on seducing me, do you?"

"Not today," he said in a light tone. "Ask me how I feel tomorrow." Daniel winked.

"Why not today," Lady Iris said. "Are you feeling indisposed for some reason?"

He turned toward her. Fury filled her gaze. She didn't like him flirting with the duchess. That was interesting... "I am not feeling my best," he confirmed. "I had a restless night."

"Nightmares?" She lifted a brow. "I must admit you don't look well." Lady Iris tilted her head to the side. "Did you drink too much?"

"No, to both questions," he replied in an amiable tone. "But I did have some dreams of the more...sensual kind." He took a bite of his eggs and chewed slowly. Daniel kept his gaze on her. "There's a woman that I can't quite forget no matter how hard I try."

"How unfortunate for the woman." She picked up the knife on her side and spread butter over her toast in a ferocious manner.

"That poor toast," he replied. "What did it do to you?"

Lady Iris opened her mouth, then closed it. She stared down at her toast and frowned. "I like it this way." She took a bite and chewed it. After she swallowed it, she grinned at him. All teeth, and a meanness in her gaze that would make a lesser man wince. Daniel was too determined to run now that he had decided upon her.

He laughed. "I think I like you," he told her. Then he turned to the other two ladies. "Do you two have any quirks like her?"

Lady Winchester shrugged. "I must admit before today I have never witnessed Iris deface toast in such a manner."

"It must be a new habit." The duchess's lips twitched as she fought a smile. "Of course it could have been brought on by frustrations of another kind."

"I do not know what you mean." Iris turned to glare at the duchess. "I'm the epitome of calm and serenity."

He adored her. "Of course you are," he said in a neutral tone. "You're definitely the epitome of something."

Lady Iris curled her fingers around the hilt of her knife. "What is that supposed to mean?"

Daniel finished his eggs instead of answering her. She was seething and it might be best not to poke her anger any more. He drank his tea and the more he sat there, his mood improved. The duchess and the countess both left. They had smiles on their faces and he couldn't help wondering if they could read the underlying tension between him and Iris.

"Why are you staring at me like that?" Iris demanded.

"You're beautiful," he said in a soft tone. "I am in awe of you."

"Well, stop it." She slammed her knife down. "I don't like it and I don't like you."

"We'll see about that." He wasn't giving up.

"No, we will not." She stood and placed her hands on the table. "You're the last man I would ever consider being with. So whatever has put that gleam in your eyes, ignore it. Whatever chance you had blew away with your cruelty."

"I'm sorry," he said in a husky tone. "I was an arse."

"Agreed," she said. "With one caveat."

He was almost afraid to ask. "And that is?"

"You're still an arse," she said in a bitter tone. "But I would have to add that you're also an arrogant arse. You think that saying you're sorry and kissing me will make me fall at your feet. As if my capitulation is a given." Her gaze went from all heat to ice in the blink of an eye. "But I won't surrender my heart to you ever again. You do not deserve me."

With those words, she left him alone. She had given him a lot to consider. Daniel wasn't even certain where to begin to make this right, but somehow he would.

Six

Iris had dressed carefully for the evening meal. It was the last night before the rest of the guests were scheduled to arrive. With Daniel, his sister, Iris and the Viscount of Goodland, they had even numbers of females to go along with the already married couples. Everyone was expected at the meal. Violet had pulled Iris aside and ordered her to attend. Francesca had been planning it for a while and she would be hurt if anyone made an excuse to stay away.

Not that Iris had planned to do anything of the sort, but she kept Francesca's feelings in mind as she prepared for the evening. She also thought about how Daniel would react. He had given her permission to use his given name and she couldn't think of him as Lord Hampstead any longer. That was far too formal, and while she would not give in to his demand to say his name, she felt justified thinking it. He didn't need to know about her little rebellion. It would only serve to make his ego grow larger than it already had.

He had inferred he dreamt about her. Perhaps he had. She certainly had dreams of him. He had haunted her far longer than she had him. She would wager her entire dowry on that. He hadn't truly noticed her before that day on Scandal Lane, and he had done a fine job of pretending she didn't exist for the past year. Nothing he said would convince her that she'd always been on his mind. Proximity had brought her to his attention, nothing more.

Tonight she wore a blue dress that matched the color of her eyes. Mary had dressed her hair so her curls were draping down her back enticingly, and sapphire pins had been added to hold them in place. Her necklace was a simple sapphire pendant shaped like a teardrop that stopped just above her chest. The overall effect was one that should appear inviting, but only with permission. Iris didn't intend to give anyone the right to touch.

She walked down the stairs slowly. Almost

everyone was in the sitting room waiting until each member of the dinner party arrived before going in to dinner. Francesca walked up beside her. "I hope you don't mind, but Lord Hampstead is leading you into dinner."

Iris frowned. That would mean she'd be required to hold a conversation with him during the meal. She gritted her teeth, but she didn't take her frustration out on her friend. "It will be all right. I promise."

"Lord Goodland will be on your other side," she said. "If it becomes too unbearable, talk to him instead."

That was not a socially acceptable move, but she might do that. Francesca had given her permission to, and this was her house and her party. "I will if I need to," she promised

"There was a tension between the two of you at breakfast," Francesca began. "Do you wish to talk about it?"

Iris shook her head. That was the last thing she wished to do. "He's being annoying, nothing more. Don't pay any attention to him or his weird behavior. I plan to."

Francesca stared at her for several moments. She did not seem convinced and honestly, Iris understood why. Daniel seemed to bring out the worst in her. She would like to reassure Francesca she could handle him; however, a part of her didn't think that was possible. Some things were left to fate and all she could do was hold on and pray she came out of it whole. "I'm trusting you," Francesca said. "And if you do need an ear to listen, don't hesitate to come to me."

"I will," she promised.

With that settled, Francesca left her alone to mingle with all her guests. After she left, Daniel came to stand beside her. "Are you going to be difficult tonight?"

"Are you going to be tedious?" she countered.

"Undoubtedly," he replied in a cool tone. "You're my dinner partner. It's inevitable."

"Then why did you bother asking me anything?" She lifted a brow. "We both know what to expect from each other." She trailed her gaze over his tall frame, from his feet all the way to his handsome face. She met his gaze and said in an acerbic tone, "You're such a disappointment."

She walked away from him before he could respond. Iris would have to spend the entire meal with him. Talking to him now would not make her want to stay for the meal. She had made a promise, and she intended to keep it. At one time, she had believed they were meant to be, but she would not make that mistake again.

Violet grabbed her arm and pulled her in close to her. "What is going on between you and Lord Hampstead," she practically hissed out the question.

"Not a thing," she said. "You don't need to worry, sister dear. I promise I have no intention of doing anything foolish." Iris had already gone down that path and she learned from her mistakes. "He frustrates me and I try to avoid him."

"Try harder," Violet told her.

Iris smiled. "I hate to tell you this, but he's my dinner companion. I can't escape him if I wanted to. Blame Francesca."

Violet groaned. "Then be polite at least."

"No promises," she replied in a amiable tone. "He brings out the worst in me. I won't make a promise I know I can't keep."

As she spoke those words, the dinner bell rang. Daniel came to her side and held out his arm. "My lady," he said in a polite tone. He was going to try to be nice. All right, she could too then.

"My lord," she said in the same polite tone. "Please, lead the way."

"My pleasure." His lips twitched.

The devil would not be able to keep this act up. She was willing to bet if she pushed hard enough, his true nature would come out before the first course. Iris held back a smile. She would have to consider what to do first.

"I don't like that look in your eyes," Daniel said. "What are you plotting?"

"You're eventual demise," she answered in a calm tone. "It is what keeps me sane."

He sighed, but she ignored it. If he hadn't wanted her to hate him, then he should have been nicer to her. The problem with it all, though, was she didn't actually despise him as much as she pretended to. He didn't need to know that part, though. Maybe one day, if he earned her trust again, she'd tell him she never stopped loving him. She prayed that day came because she didn't want to completely give up on him.

"What can I do to stop this animosity between us?" he asked. They neared the table. When they reached their designated seats, he pulled out her chair for her. When she was seated, he leaned down and said, "Because while this is quite stimulating...I want a different kind of passion between us."

Iris clenched her teeth together. "You'll wait a very long time for that."

"I do not believe I will," he said as he slid into his own seat. "The dance has already begun."

He was so sure of himself. The bastard... Well, she wasn't ready to give up. He had a lesson or two to learn, and she had the perfect way to teach him one. She grinned and turned to Lord Goodland. "My lord," she began. "Could you help me with something?" She batted her eyelashes at him in a way she prayed was flirtatious.

WHAT THE HELL GAME WAS SHE TRYING TO PLAY AT now? She ignored him throughout dinner. Not once had she turned to him. His Iris was flirting quite openly with Goodland and if his friend didn't stop responding, he was going to have to beat him bloody.

"I've always found dreams a prelude to the real thing," Goodland began. "A good one prepares you for the genuine pleasure that awaits you."

"Is that so?" Iris said, leaning a little closer. "Tell me about your last dream."

Bloody hell... Daniel clenched his fork in his

hand. His knuckles were white as he fought the rage building inside of him. Goodland better not answer that question truthfully.

"I haven't dreamed anything substantial in quite some time," Goodland answered. "There's been a lack of inspiration of late."

Goodland turned to the lady on his other side, Daniel's sister, Lady Calliope. "What about you?" he asked her. "What do you think of dreams?"

"Dreams are a wonderful way for us to imagine what we have trouble reaching in our waking moments. It's like a wish brought forward, but one we don't dare to achieve."

"That's lovely," Goodland said in a warm tone.

Thank God they were on the last course. Goodland was flirting with Iris and Daniel's sister. He was going to kill him. There was no way around it. He didn't want to do it. Goodland was a good friend to have, but he was going too far. Both Iris and Calliope were out of his league. Especially since he made it clear that he would never marry, and he wanted his family's title to die with him. He had a lot of hatred for his father.

They finished the last course. Everyone stood. "Ladies," the duchess began. "If you'll join me in the sitting room for after-dinner drinks." She smiled at them. "Gentlemen, follow my husband to the game room. I believe he has something special planned for you all."

They separated and went to their designated rooms. Daniel wanted to pull Iris aside and kiss her senseless. It wasn't the time or place for it. Besides, he had to deal with Goodland first. They went into the game room. Lindsey poured them all snifters of brandy and passed them out. "Now that dinner is over, the real fun can begin."

"What did you have in mind?" Winchester asked. "It's been a long day."

"You're an old married man now," Goodland said, then laughed. "You can stay here longer. We don't have the opportunity to gather together like this anymore."

"He's right," Merrifield said. "Some of us are old married men now. With wives waiting in a warm bed." He laughed at the stricken look on Goodland's face.

"Don't rub it in," Goodland said. "Some of us have a cold bed."

"You can fix that, you know," Lindsey said. "Find a woman willing to put up with you and you'll always have that warm bed."

"No, thank you," Goodland said. "I will have

another snifter of brandy though." He held out his glass for Lindsey to pour brandy into it.

"We're going to play a drinking game." Lindsey grinned. There was a devilish glint in his gaze that Daniel didn't like. Sometimes the duke could be truly wicked. "The loser has to drink each hand they lose."

Merrifield groaned. "I don't want to go to bed foxed. Violet won't appreciate that." The marquess had settled into marriage far better than Daniel had believed he would. They all had been so adamant against it. Why did any of them think they could avoid marriage he didn't understand. They were so determined to remain bachelors. Daniel was contemplating taking that step. He knew he wanted Iris, and if he wanted her forever he would have to marry her. Convincing her of that would be the hard part. For tonight he wanted to forget all that though. He'd play this game the duke had in mind. What did he have to lose?

Daniel didn't care how much he had to drink. He did not have a wife to worry about. If Iris were waiting for him, he might object to this game, but as she wasn't, he said, "I'm in."

They all settled down at the table. They were playing Faro. Merrifield didn't do well with any card game, but luck was usually on Daniel's side. Which was why he couldn't help being surprised by how many times he'd lost. "Are these cards rigged?"

"Would I do that?" Lindsey said and held his hand on his chest. "You wound me."

He had already drank more than half the decanter of brandy. The room was blurry as hell. Daniel narrowed his gaze. "You're up to something." He slurred his words. "I don't know what, but I will figure it out."

Goodland slapped him on the back. "You're paranoid, my friend."

Daniel glared at him. He forgot to speak to him about his flirting earlier. "You need to stay away from my sister." He had no claim on Iris. Yet. But he could warn him off of Calliope.

"I had to escort her in to dinner. Did you want me to be rude to her?" Goodland shook his head, then played his card. Daniel cursed. He had lost this hand.

"Give me the brandy," he conceded, his loss. Lindsey poured it into his snifter, and that was the end of that decanter. "We're out of brandy."

"Don't worry," Lindsey said. "There is more."

"I can't drink any more." He was done for the

night. If he drank another sip he might fall into unconsciousness. "I'm going to bed."

Daniel stood and swayed a little on his feet. Damn, he was stupid drunk. Why had he agreed to this game again?

"Can you even make it up the stairs?" Merrifield asked.

"Of course I can," he insisted. He walked, what he thought, was a straight line to the door. He heard laughs behind him, but he didn't turn and glare at them. If he did, he might fall over and he was determined to make it to his bedchamber.

Somehow, by some miracle, he fumbled his way up the stairs and into his bedchamber. He didn't bother with lighting a candle or calling for his valet. All he wanted to do was crawl into bed and sleep off the brandy. Daniel yanked off his boots and tossed them to the side, then slid off his jacket and waistcoat. When he had all of his clothes off, he slid into bed completely naked and then curled up against the warm body next to him. He didn't question why she was there. She visited his dreams so often he assumed she was there to return to her nightly haunting...

Seven

Heat spread over Iris in waves. She tried to push the blanket off of her, but it was too heavy, almost intractable. Dreams filled her mind. He was there. He was always there. She reached for him and held on. Only in this world could she give in and touch him the way she wanted to. Iris couldn't forget about him. Would never forget about him... But giving in to her deepest desire was not something she could do in reality.

This dream seemed more real than any of the others. His skin underneath her fingers was hot, hard, and sensuous. How could her mind have brought so much detail in where it had failed before? She should open her eye and escape from this fantasy, but she wanted more. Iris wanted to press herself up against him. To taste his lips against hers and touch more of his body that was so different from hers. She needed to do that almost as much as she needed to take her next breath.

Iris curled against the heat. Where she had been ready to remove it a few moments earlier, now she craved it. His hand moved over her hip and cupped her bottom. It was like a brand that was now permanently etched on her skin. When his lips finally came down on hers, she moaned.

She wrapped her arms around him. This... Iris lost all ability to think. She had been on the brink of a revelation, but he had slid his hand lower. Her dressing gown slid upward, and then he pushed his hand upward. Confusion filled her mind. She'd never taken things this far in her dreams. In truth, she had never taken him to her bed in them. They had kissed, and kissed, and kissed. But nothing more... This dream had taken on a life of its own.

He brushed his fingers over her spine, then slid them in between her legs. When he brushed them over her sex, she gasped. It was so intimate and taboo. She should not let him touch her this way. Iris had to wake up and stop this dream. Even if it was a temptation, she found irresistible. She would never be able to meet his gaze and not think of this delectably stunning dream.

Iris pulled away from the kiss. He didn't like that and pulled her against him again. Daniel didn't want to let her out of the dream anymore than Iris wished to go. She had to do it, though. "No," she said in a husky tone. "We can't. It's..."

She didn't finish the sentence. His mouth came back down on hers. The kiss stole her breath with its intensity. His fingers slid against the sensitive nub between her legs, over and over again in a rhythm so sensual it made her moan. Daniel slid his tongue into her mouth and tangled it with hers in an inti-mate dance. The kiss along with the motions of his fingers, was too much. Something was building up inside of her. There was an intense pressure and only he could make her reach the peak that would send her over. She pressed herself against him and writhed with each slide of his fingers over her.

Iris would have screamed if he didn't swallow it with a kiss. Her eyes flew open. Somewhere along the way she had realized that she hadn't been dreaming, but she hadn't wanted to admit it. There was no denying it now. That was not something her mind could have imagined.

She scraped her nails against his naked flesh.

"Daniel," she said in a harsh whisper. His eyes were closed, and he was unresponsive. He leaned into her and trailed kisses along her neck and down to her bosom. He sucked on her breast, pulling the nipple into his mouth through the cloth of her dressing gown. Iris moaned. She cursed under her breath. He had to stop, but damn if she wanted to let him have his way with her. He'd already gone too far, anyway. Why not take this act to its inevitable conclusion?

"You feel so good," he said in a gravelly voice. "So, so good."

Iris groaned. He felt damn good, too. "Daniel," she tried saying his name again.

"Yes, love," he said in a tone that made her entire body shiver. "Say my name. Say it for me again. I've been dying to hear it from your lips."

He was going to be the death of her. "Daniel," she said more sharply. Iris didn't know why he was in her bed, but he had to leave. Before her maid came in and then there would be no turning back. So far no one knew he had been in here. They were safe from this ruinous act. But only if he left soon.

His eyelids fluttered open, and he met her gaze. He hummed a little in pleasure. "I don't know why you're in my bed, but I'm so glad you're here."

She frowned. "Are you drunk?"

"No," he said. "Well, I might have been."

Great. He had crawled into her bed completely foxed and unaware of what he had been doing. She wanted to smack him. "I am not in your bed," she said in an irritated tone. "You are in my bed, you sodding fool."

"What?" He jerked upward and stared down at her. He was finally blinking away the remnants of sleep. "Iris?"

She sighed. He was as confused as she had been. The pleasure he had given her had been intense, but she also realized that it would lead somewhere she couldn't go. He didn't want to marry anyone, especially her. He had made his feelings for her very clear. It did not matter how she felt about him. Iris could not risk finding herself in a precarious position. If she were to end up with child... She shook her head away. They had not gone that far in this farce. She was safe from being tied to this man for the rest of her life.

DANIEL STARED DOWN AT HER, SHOCK FILLING HIM. What the hell had happened. He was in bed with her and he could not discern how he had come to be with her. How much brandy had he drank? She stared up at him as if he'd grown two heads. His cock was hard as a rock, even with that look of disapproval on her face. Her lips were plump from his kisses.

Bloody hell...

He had been touching her, kissing her, and so close to spreading her legs to shove himself inside of her. He still wanted to do that. She was there and it would be easy to seduce her, and love her the way he had been dreaming for days.

But that would be wrong.

His Iris deserved to be courted properly. As it was, he already ruined her by being in her bed. The sun would rise soon and if he were caught there... A courtship would not happen. He would have to marry her. There would be no choice for either one of them. He wanted her to have that choice, and he wanted her to choose to be with him.

"You need to leave," she hissed out.

"I know," he said. His heart hurt. Daniel rubbed his chest, hoping to ease that pain. What the hell had he done? "I'm..." He had been about to tell her he was sorry, but he didn't get the words out.

In that moment, he realized two things. He was

completely naked, and Iris hadn't stopped him from kissing her or from bringing her to climax. Why had she allowed it to go as far as she had? He narrowed his gaze. "Iris," he began. He was suddenly uncertain if he hadn't taken her completely. "Did we?"

She shook her head. "We can talk about this later. When you're dressed and not in my bedchamber."

But he had to know, or he would dwell on it until he saw her next. Daniel would have to make some decisions regardless, but he couldn't make proper ones without all the information. "Tell me," he insisted.

Iris groaned and that just make his cock harder. She had made some delectable noises as he had pleasured her. He was certain of that much. They were imprinted on his brain. "Why are you so difficult?"

"This conversation could already have been over," he told her. "You're the one delaying the answer."

She shook her head. There was some light coming through the window now. Not a lot. Just enough for him to make out the blush that had creeped up her neck and settled into her cheeks.

She was adorable. "We did not..." She blew out a breath and waved her hand. "...complete it."

He grinned. "I didn't shove my cock between your legs and take your innocence." He said the words to shock her. Daniel had a perverse notion to see if she could blush more than she already had. He was delighted to discover her cheeks could stain a brighter shade of pink.

"No," she forced the word out. "Now can you please leave."

"I'll have to dress first," he told her. "I can't walk out of here naked. It would be quite scandalous."

She pinned him with a gaze so menacing it should have terrified him. Instead, it made him laugh. Iris smacked him. "Get out of my bed."

"If you insist," he said in a casual tone. Daniel slipped out of the bed, not bothering to cover himself. He bent over and started picking up his scattered clothing.

She gasped. "Do you have no shame?"

Daniel glanced over his shoulder and smiled. "Should I?" He winked.

Iris stared at him. She might be scandalized, but she did not look away. While he dressed, and he did it as slow as possible, she kept her gaze on him. She tracked each movement and almost seemed disappointed when he was fully dressed. Daniel slid his boots on and then stood to stare at her. "Did you enjoy that?"

"I did," she said. "If I have to be accosted in my own bedchamber, I should have something in return."

"I would say your climax was gift enough," he drawled.

Her mouth fell open as if she was going to disagree. "As nice as this was. You should already be out of my room and in your own."

Daniel grinned. "I'm glad you enjoyed it. Perhaps next time we both can come out of it as happy."

"You're such a scoundrel," she said in an exasperated tone. "This is not happening ever again."

"We'll see," he replied with a hint of roguishness in his voice. "I'm glad you've given in and decided to use my given name." He bowed. "I'll see you at breakfast."

Daniel turned to exit her bedchamber. When he opened the door, he froze. Standing outside of her chamber about to knock was Iris's sister, Violet.

"Lord Hampstead," she said, then frowned. "I thought this was Iris's chamber."

He stood there like a fool, not sure how to answer. Should he pretend she had the wrong room? Would she even believe that? What would happen if she left in search of the right room, only to discover she had the correct one all along? He cursed under his breath. Violet looked past him and met Iris's gaze.

"I see," she said in a concerned tone, then stepped aside. "Go to your own bedchamber. I will talk to you later. Right now, I need to speak with my sister."

Daniel glanced over at Iris, then at her sister. He wanted to stay and help her. It was his bad, inebriated decision that landed him in her bed. The entire situation was his fault, and he should own up to it.

"Go," Iris told him. "Now is not the time for you to pretend you're a gentleman and not a scoundrel."

The muscles in his cheek twitched at her words. They would talk about this later, but for now he would heed to her wishes. She belonged to him, and she would realize that sooner rather than later. Whether she liked it or not. They were bound together now. There would be no turning back.

Eight

Violet turned around and stared at Iris. Heat crept up her neck and settled into her cheeks. Her sister was going to lecture her, and there would be no avoiding any second of it. Iris couldn't slip past Violet and run away as much as she would like to. She was still wearing her bedclothes and she couldn't very well leave her bed chamber yet. There was only one thing she could do.

Iris slid out of bed and pulled the bell to summon her maid. She would have Mary come in and help her dress. It would help to keep her lecture to a minimum. Violet wouldn't want to spill too many details with the maid in the room with them. Hopefully, it would not take long for Mary to arrive.

"Are you going to say anything for yourself?" Violet demanded. She folded her arms over her chest and glared at Iris.

"What would you like me to say?" She lifted a brow. "You've already decided as to what you believe happened. You always make assumptions and then think you need to tell me what I should do. So," Iris said in a noncommittal tone. "Why don't we get that part over with and I can go about my day."

"How can you be so flippant about this?" Violet's voice took on a shrill tone that was ear piercing in its intensity. "You were in bed and a gentleman was leaving your room. Why are you acting as if nothing of import happened?"

Because nothing had... Daniel would have done all of that with any woman. She was a convenient, warm body next to him. He had fallen into her bed in a drunken stupor, and when he found a woman at his side, he decided seduction would be a good idea. Iris would not let that determine how she would live the rest of her life. Even if the pleasure had been overwhelming and she would remember it for the rest of her life. "Why are you acting as if you walked in on us in the middle of a good tumble?" Iris rolled her eyes. "Lord Hampstead did not take my virtue. He entered my room by mistake."

Iris had to pray that her sister took her word for that. In truth, he hadn't taken her virginity. She was untouched, but she would never be the same. He had loved her with his hands and his mouth, and if attempted to seduce her, she might not be able to say no. Iris knew that if she allowed him to have his way with her, the pleasure would go beyond her imagination.

"How long was he in here?" Violet asked.

"I cannot say," Iris said. "I was asleep when he entered and don't know how long he was in here before I was aware of his presence." That was the absolute truth. She had been dreaming of him and that fantasy world had bled into reality. It turned out the real thing was far better, and she hadn't wanted it to end.

"You promise he didn't seduce you?" Violet said in a firm tone.

Iris met her sister's gaze. "I would not lie to you about my virtue. You do not need to demand Lord Hampstead ask for my hand. I do not require you to secure me a husband."

Violet sighed. "I don't like this. If anyone else had come in here..."

"If you hadn't come to my room when you had, no one else would know. I shouldn't be punished for Lord Hampstead's inability to know what door opens to his bedchamber." She jutted her chin out in defiance. "I am not marrying that man."

"Even to save your reputation?" Violet tilted her head to the side. "I don't understand. This was something you wanted at one time. What changed?"

"I was a naive girl then." She hadn't known how Lord Hampstead had felt about her. "I thought I could make him love me. No one can make anyone feel emotions they lack inside of them. The earl can't love me and I won't marry a man that will grow to resent me. I'm glad I never went through with that foolish plan."

Violet nodded. "I understand and I won't insist you do something you're adamantly against." She bit her bottom lip. "But Iris..."

"No," Iris interrupted her. "Do not finish that sentence. No one will know about this unless we say something. I don't plan on mentioning the earl wandered into my bedchamber. You hold your tongue too and I won't be forced into an unwanted marriage."

Violet was quiet for several moments, then she

met Iris's gaze and nodded. "I am going to tell Zachariah. I can't keep secrets from my husband. But he won't tell anyone else. Lord Hampstead is his friend too and he won't want either of you to suffer consequences from an innocent mistake."

Iris didn't want Violet's husband to know about any of it, but she also understood why she didn't want to keep a secret from him. "All right," she conceded. "I am placing my trust in you and your husband's discretion."

"You can rely on me. I've never let you down in the past, have I?"

Violet had always been a wonderful sister. Her twin had been the one person who Iris could rely on and she didn't expect that would change now. "No," Iris agreed. "It's not you I'm unsure of. Your husband isn't someone I've known my entire life. I don't want him to think ill of me."

"You're not the one in the wrong here." Violet frowned. "Unless there is something you're not telling me. Did you invite Lord Hampstead into your bedchamber?"

Iris snorted. "Definitely not." She had been actively avoiding the earl since she arrived for the house party. "I do not wish to disrupt my entire life for someone as unreliable as the Earl of Hampstead."

"Then you do not need to concern yourself with my husband's opinion of you. It would be his friend he may take offense with." Violet blew out a breath. "I'll leave you be for now. Mary will be here soon to help you dress. When you're finished, meet me in the sitting room. Francesca requested we join her there before we break our fast."

Iris nodded. "Thank you."

"There're no thanks necessary. You're my sister. I wouldn't harm you for any reason." Violet hugged her and then left the room.

Iris stood there alone for several seconds, fighting tears. A part of her wanted to believe Daniel's kisses and his touch had meant something to him, too. She wouldn't allow herself to feel anymore for him or wish he could be something he was incapable of being. It was far better to pretend he hadn't touched her so intimately. Somehow she didn't think she could ever forget, though...

DANIEL COULD NOT BELIEVE WHAT HE HAD DONE. Oh, he had enjoyed every second of it, but he should not have touched her. Now he couldn't get her out of his head. The touch of her silken skin and the moans that had echoed through the room as she climaxed.

Bloody hell...

He would never be able to forget those moments when she was pressed against him. Daniel craved her like a thirsty man craved his next drink. He had become addicted to her in a short time. His imagination had not done her justice. Now he wanted to march back up the stairs and strip her naked, then taste every inch of her. Daniel wanted to take everything she offered and give all he had of himself to her. Only her.

But he feared she would shut him out. He had already taken too much from her that she hadn't freely given. How could he possibly make her understand he hadn't meant to crawl into her bed, and that he would not have consciously touched her without her permission? She might never forgive him, as much as he enjoyed being with her in that bed, the moment of pleasure was not worth losing her forever.

When he had first woke beside her, he had been amused. Now that he was thinking clearer, he knew it had not been a good thing. Facing her after that would be one of the hardest things he ever had to do. She would probably come down to breakfast soon. Which was why he was in the library instead of eating. His stomach wouldn't be able to handle food, anyway.

"There you are," Merrifield said from the entrance.

Daniel glanced at the marquess. "Did you need me for something?" He hadn't been hiding, exactly. The library had seemed like a better option than the breakfast room He'd hoped to avoid upsetting Iris. After he had washed and changed in his bedchamber, which ironically was located next to Iris's, he'd decided to avoid her for as long as possible. Admittedly, that wasn't very courageous of him; however, he never claimed to be brave.

"Yes," Merrifield began. His tone was infused with anger. "I want you to explain yourself."

For a brief moment, Daniel was surprised, and almost asked what he needed to clarify for him. Then he grasped the reason for his anger, and the demand. How the hell had Merrifield found out already? Then he recalled that the marquess was married to Iris's sister. "What would you like for me to tell you?" He was being obstinate, but he didn't care for the way Merrifield looked at him.

"I want you to tell me that you did not touch

Lady Iris Keene," he said. His tone went ice cold. "That I do not have to explain to my wife that one of my closest friends is the scoundrel the ton believe him to be."

The muscles in his cheeks twitched. He couldn't tell Merrifield that because he *had* touched Iris. He had stroked her in ways a man who was not her husband should have, then kissed her until he swallowed her screams of pleasure. What was far worse...he wanted to do it all over again, then repeat it until they were both sated and worn out from their loving.

The marquess met his gaze, then cursed under his breath. He knew without Daniel saying a word that he couldn't say the words he needed him to. "I didn't take her virtue," he told his friend. "She isn't tainted by me." Not completely anyway.

"But you're not as innocent as she led Violet to believe." Merrifield clenched his hands into a fist. "You did do something inappropriate."

"If that is the standard we are using," Daniel began. "I've done many things that could be considered unseemly." He met the marquess's gaze. "Lady Iris and I have kissed, and more than once." That was the complete truth. "The first time was over a year ago. When I retrieved her from the wooded path on Scandal Lane." He shrugged. "So, yes, I did do something unsuitable, and I'm not going to even try to make any justification for my actions." He didn't have any that would exonerate him. Daniel had acted improperly and deserved his friend's derision.

Merrifield didn't say a word. He stepped forward and his fist hit Daniel's face before he realized the marquess had raised his arm. Daniel fell to the ground and his head hit the floor hard.

"Get up," Merrifield demanded.

Daniel moved spit blood out of his mouth. He had bitten his tongue when Merrifield's fist made contact. He moved his jaw around and winced. "I will not fight you." He met his friend's gaze. "I'll allow I deserve to take that punch, but I refuse to let you have a second one."

He didn't want to hurt his friend, but he would if he had to. Daniel crawled up and used a table to help him stand. If the marquess knew about what had happened, that meant that Iris and Violet were done talking. Iris hadn't told Violet everything, but she must have come to her own conclusions. If Merrifield knew everything, he would have hit him first and asked questions later.

"That's too bad," Merrifield said. "Because I

am not done with you."

He took another swing at Daniel; however, this time he was prepared for it and ducked. Merrifield fell forward and jammed his knee on the table. He cursed and turned toward Daniel again.

"Stop," Daniel said. "You do not need to protect her reputation."

"Why the hell not? Do you believe she's not worth protecting?" Merrifield glared at him.

"She's worth everything," Daniel said in a determined tone. "I don't need you to make me do anything. I know what needs to be done."

Merrifield stared at him for several seconds then said, "See that it is done today." With those words, he left Daniel alone. He sighed and slumped into a chair. He had some decisions to make and a lady to track down. But first he wanted a moment to just breathe...

Iris didn't want breakfast. After her meeting with her sister and Francesca in the sitting room, she went to the library instead. The morning had been tumultuous and exhausting, and she didn't want to face the rest of the guests in attendance.

She would go to her bedchamber, but there were too many memories there haunting the room. The library had those two, but they were not as intense. She didn't know how she was going to sleep in that room ever again. Whenever she closed her eyes, all she would be able to see was him and the way his hand felt gliding across her skin. She nearly moaned again at the memory of that pleasure.

When she reached the library, she walked inside, then halted immediately. Daniel sat on a chair with his eyes closed. His lip was swollen and there was a slight bruise forming on his cheek. She moved over to him and demanded, "What happened to you?"

His eyelids fluttered open. There was an intensity in his gaze that stole her breath. "Hello, Iris," he said in a tone so husky it sent shivers down her spine.

It hadn't slipped past her that he hadn't answered his question. She moved closer to him and reached out to touch his lip, but then thought better of it and pulled her hand back. "Who did that to you?"

He brought his hand up and covered his mouth with his fingers. "It's nothing." He smiled. "If you're worried you can do something to help."

His charm was pouring out of him like a storm

descending upon the earth, drenching it with its torrential rain. It washed over her so fast and hard she couldn't evade it, even if she wanted to. Iris didn't want to avoid him. She was tired of running from her own feelings. "And what is that?" She lifted a brow.

Daniel tapped his lip. "Kiss it and make it all better."

Iris grinned. She had a feeling the scoundrel would say something outlandish. "I am not sure that would help you." She crossed her arms over her chest. "I believe you will be all right and you do not need me."

He leaned forward and fell to his knees before Iris. "That's where you're wrong."

She stared down at him. "What are you doing?"

Her heart started to beat heavily inside of her chest. He had a look in his eyes that set her blood on fire and it made her want things she crushed down inside of her for fear they would never be hers. She swallowed hard and tried to step back.

Daniel reached for her and pulled her close to him. He kept his arms wrapped around her legs. She pressed her hands to his shoulders, intending to push him away from her, but something inside of her told her to wait.

"Iris," he said in an imploring tone. "Don't go. I need you more than I can possibly put into words."

"Try," she insisted. "I cannot make myself believe you want me or if you even need me."

"Oh," he began. "I want you and," he said as he met her gaze. "I most definitely need you."

She rolled her eyes. Part of her wanted to tell him to prove it, but she didn't require that show of faith from him. He had demonstrated his desire for her quite efficiently in her bed a few hours ago. "I don't believe you," she said in a whispered tone. Her heart was in her throat.

"From the first moment, when your lips touched mine, I knew that you were the only woman I could or would ever need." His gaze didn't waver as he spoke. "Until that day I was lost, and it terrified me because you had such a hold on me. I pushed you away when I should have been pulling you closer. I'm sorry." He was quiet for a moment, then said in a pleading tone, "Please forgive me."

She wanted to say there was nothing to forgive. To slide her fears away as if they meant nothing. "I want to." It would be so easy to fall into his arms and accept everything he was saying. If she hoped to have a relationship with him, she needed honesty from him.

"I understand." He leaned his head against her stomach. "I don't deserve it."

Tears threatened to fall from her eyes. She fought them because she hated crying in front of anyone, and it would hurt even more in front of him. "Forgiveness is easy," she told him. "It's forgetting that is more difficult."

He didn't move for a few seconds. She brushed her fingers through his hair. When he lifted his head to meet her gaze. "I want every day to feel the way it feels when I am with you. If you will allow me a chance, I promise to ensure that you never have a reason to doubt me again."

"What are you asking?" she said in a raspy tone.

"Marry me," he said. "Let this be the beginning of our forever and spend the rest of our days discovering where the rest of our story goes."

She never imagined she would hear those words from him, and she still couldn't quite believe he said them to her now. This time she couldn't stop the tear from falling down her cheek. She wiped it away quickly, then nodded. "Yes," she said. "A thousand times, yes."

He stood and pulled her into his arms. When he

kissed her this time, she didn't question it. Instead, she allowed herself to become lost in it. Because once she'd fallen in love with her scoundrel, she had known where she belonged. Her foolish pride had made her want to fight it, fight him. She was done with that absurd behavior. Daniel was hers, and she'd always been his.

One year later…

Iris sat in the sitting room at Hampstead House. It had been a year since Daniel had proposed to her. She had gone into her marriage full of hope mixed with apprehension. There was nothing she wanted more than to believe everything Daniel had said to her that day, and for the most part she had. That didn't mean she didn't still hold some reservations about her future happiness. How could she not have? Daniel had hurt her and pushed her away too many times for her not to have any doubts.

Thankfully all those fears had been for nothing. Daniel was the best husband, and more than she could have hoped for. The past year had been so wonderful she couldn't believe she had ever hesitated to say yes to his proposal. Now she had something to tell him. Some big news she'd been holding inside until she knew for certain.

Daniel walked into the sitting room. He smiled at her, then walked over to her in long strides. "Hello, love," he said before he leaned down and pressed his lips to hers. "You're beautiful."

Heat filled her cheeks. She should be used to this by now, but he still set her heart aflutter with a few simple words and a brief kiss hello. How had she gotten so lucky. "I missed you this morning," she said. "And last night."

He had gone away overnight to see to some estate business. "I missed you more," he said. "At least you had the comfort of our bed to keep you warm."

"It's not all that warm without you in it," she informed him. Then sighed. "But you're here. How's the property?"

He blew out a breath. "It's part of Calliope's dowry. Someone was interested in purchasing it, but I declined. She may want to use it for something else."

"Oh?" Iris lifted a brow. "What would your sister use property for?"

"Herself," he said, then shrugged. "She doesn't have to marry. I already put the deed in her name, though I won't tell her that just yet. I want her to have choices."

"How sweet," she said. "Why do you think marriage is so terrible." Iris raised a brow. "Are you not happy you've married me?"

"Darling," he said in a soothing tone. "Not all marriages are like ours."

Iris grinned. He was right of course but she had to make a point or he'd be insufferable. "I don't know. I can name three marriages besides ours that have worked out splendidly."

"Our friends do not count…" He shook his head. "Each situation is not the norm. You know that."

She patted the seat next to her. "We have all made everything more difficult than it had to be. Each one of us has been stubborn, and yet, we have all found a way around it to love. It might not be the norm, but it isn't unusual either. Callie could find love. Don't discount her appeal to the gentlemen of the ton." Lady Calliope Andrews had gorgeous blonde hair and brilliant blue eyes, and a face that would make men stop in their tracks. She would be surrounded by eligible gentlemen of the ton. Iris was certain of that, and Daniel would have to weed through them. There would be some fortune hunters that circled her too. Calliope probably wouldn't even notice them though. She had her sight set on a particular gentleman. Iris would bet everything on that fact.

He sighed. "That's also something I fear." Daniel leaned back. "But I'll have to deal with it. She's got a whole list of balls she wishes to be escorted to. I hope you're ready to help with that."

"Callie is a dear," Iris said. "It won't be that much of a chore."

Daniel's sister was excited. Iris could remember when she'd been that way once upon a time. What Iris didn't say to her husband though…Callie seemed particularly interested in the Viscount of Goodland—one of Daniel's closest friends. She was fairly certain that he wouldn't be happy with that pairing. He loved Goodland, and he loved his sister, but he would not love them together.

"Let's put that aside to worry about another day," she said after she shook those thoughts away. "I've something to tell you."

"What?" he said in a wary tone.

"Don't think the worst," she said and laughed. "It's good news. I promise." She was so giddy with happiness. Daniel would feel that too, along with the fears. She'd help him through it all.

He pulled her into his lap and nuzzled his neck. "Then tell me so I can stop imagining the worst." Her poor, poor Daniel. Always thinking of everything that could go wrong instead of the possibilities.

Iris took his hand and pressed it to her belly. "We're going to have a baby."

His eyes widened. "You're certain?" His voice cracked as he spoke.

"I estimate I'm three months along," she said. "I'm as certain as can be."

She had suspected a month ago, but hadn't wanted to jinx anything. She had seen a doctor while Daniel was away. With her pregnancy confirmed she was confident she could tell him the news. He could be more anxious than her at times. He'd probably be a little insane throughout her pregnancy. He would hate the thought of losing her. She'd have to reassure him all along until the babe was born.

He hugged her close. "I love you," he said in a

hoarse whisper. He met hr gaze. "More and more every day."

She pulled back and cupped his cheeks in her hands. "I love you too." Then she leaned into him and pressed her lips to his. The kiss was sweet and full love all the love they shared. This was the life she'd always wanted, had imagined, and felt incredibly blessed to have. If something is meant to be, it will be, and she thanked heaven every day that her and Daniel were together as they should be.

Thank you so much for taking the time to read my book.

Your opinion matters!

Please take a moment to review this book on your favorite review site and share your opinion with fellow readers.

www.authordawnbrower.com

Acknowledgments

Special thanks to Elizabeth Evans. Your encouragement and assistance with this book helped me immensely. I am grateful for all you do for me.

About Dawn Brower

USA TODAY Bestselling author, DAWN BROWER writes both historical and contemporary romance. There are always stories inside her head; she just never thought she could make them come to life. That creativity has finally found an outlet.

Growing up, she was the only girl out of six children. She raised two boys as a single mother; there is never a dull moment in her life. Reading books is her favorite hobby, and she loves all genres.

www.authordawnbrower.com
TikTok: @1DawnBrower

BB bookbub.com/authors/dawn-brower

f facebook.com/1DawnBrower

twitter.com/1DawnBrower

instagram.com/1DawnBrower

g goodreads.com/dawnbrower

Also by Dawn Brower

HISTORICAL

Stand alone:

Broken Pearl

A Wallflower's Christmas Kiss

A Gypsy's Christmas Kiss

Marsden Romances

A Flawed Jewel

A Crystal Angel

A Treasured Lily

A Sanguine Gem

A Hidden Ruby

A Discarded Pearl

Marsden Descendants

Rebellious Angel

Tempting An American Princess

How to Kiss a Debutante

Loving an America Spy

Linked Across Time

Saved by My Blackguard

Searching for My Rogue

Seduction of My Rake

Surrendering to My Spy

Spellbound by My Charmer

Stolen by My Knave

Separated from My Love

Scheming with My Duke

Secluded with My Hellion

Secrets of My Beloved

Spying on My Scoundrel

Shocked by My Vixen

Smitten with My Christmas Minx

Vision of Love

Enduring Legacy

The Legacy's Origin

Charming Her Rogue

Ever Beloved

Forever My Earl

Always My Viscount

Infinitely My Marquess

Eternally My Duke

Bluestockings Defying Rogues

When An Earl Turns Wicked

A Lady Hoyden's Secret

One Wicked Kiss

Earl In Trouble

All the Ladies Love Coventry

One Less Scandalous Earl

Confessions of a Hellion

The Vixen in Red

Lady Pear's Duke

Scandal Meets Love

Love Only Me (Amanda Mariel)

Find Me Love (Dawn Brower)

If It's Love (Amanda Mariel)

Odds of Love (Dawn Brower)

Believe In Love (Amanda Mariel)

Chance of Love (Dawn Brower)

Love and Holly (Amanda Mariel)

Love and Mistletoe (Dawn Brower

The Neverhartts

Never Defy a Vixen

Never Disregard a Wallflower

Never Dare a Hellion

Never Deceive a Bluestocking

Never Disrespect a Governess

Never Desire a Duke

CONTEMPORARY

Stand alone:

Deadly Benevolence

Snowflake Kisses

Kindred Lies

Sparkle City

Diamonds Don't Cry

Hooking a Firefly

Novak Springs

Cowgirl Fever

Dirty Proof

Unbridled Pursuit

Sensual Games

Christmas Temptation

Daring Love

Passion and Lies

Desire and Jealousy

Seduction and Betrayal

Begin Again

There You'll Be

Better as a Memory

Won't Let Go

Heart's Intent

One Heart to Give

Unveiled Hearts

Heart of the Moment

Kiss My Heart Goodbye

Heart in Waiting

Heart Lessons

A Heart Redeemed

Excerpt: When I Loved a Charmer

SCANDALOUS GENTLEMEN BOOK FOUR

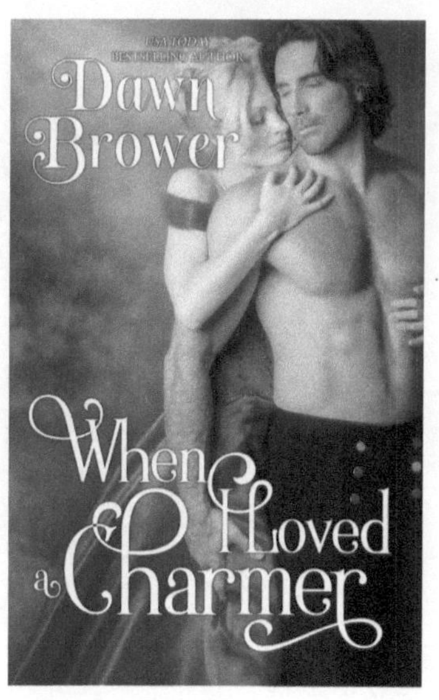

Calliope was on a mission, and she refused to accept defeat. She would attend the Christmastide house party, and her brother would agree. She had to go. She just *had* to, because if she didn't, then she might not be a social success. "Daniel?" Calliope said as she entered her brother's study. She was a little apprehensive because he could be cross when interrupted.

"Yes, Calliope?" He lifted his gaze to meet hers. He rubbed his temples a little absentmindedly. His head must ache. She would have to be quick and leave. She hated how hard he worked. Her brother didn't seem happy to her, and she wanted him to be.

She walked to front of his desk and stood there with her hands behind her back. She was pretty sure she knew what he saw when he looked at her. Daniel didn't want to think of her as a grown woman. But she was now and he had to accept that. She had golden blonde curls that were pinned on top of her head, but most of it was plaited and twisted into a chignon. Her day dress was a cornflower blue that matched her eyes. She wanted a husband, and a life that wasn't lived inside her childhood home.

"About the invitation to the Christmastide..."

"No," he interrupted her. His tone was firm and harsh. That was not a good sign. She barely held back a sigh of irritation. He met her gaze and told her, "We are not going."

"Please," Calliope said in a pleading tone. "It'll help me. In a few months I'll have my come out and this will give me a chance to learn some of the social skills I'll need. These are people you socialize with regularly, isn't it? Why don't you want to go?" She didn't understand her brother's reluctance to socialize. Did he really think some young miss would somehow force him to marry. Calliope wished he would marry someone. He'd probably be less irritable if he did.

Daniel pinched the bridge of his nose. His pain must have worsened. She bit he lip pensively as she waited for him to answer. "I hate Christmastide," he reminded her.

She pouted. Calliope hated that she had to act like a spoiled child to make him listen to her. "Then be grumpy the entire time. It is what you do every year, anyway." Calliope placed her palms on his desk and met his gaze. "I want my season to be successful. Please don't be difficult and help me."

Calliope would be eight and ten in a month, and her first season would be, soon. The Christmastide party was informal, and she had been invited along with him. He had to see how it would be beneficial for her. She could become more acquainted with the Duchess of Lindsey, the hostess of the event, and that connection at her back she would be nearly guaranteed a success.

He appeared to think about what she said. He sighed. "I'll consider it," he told her.

She rolled her eyes. "Consider fast. We will have to depart London soon if we're going to travel to the Duke of Lindsey's home in the country."

"Is that so?" He fought a smile. "I hadn't realized that. If you need an answer now, I believe I already gave you one." He could be such an arse sometimes…

She held back the retort she was about to spit back at him, but couldn't hold in the groan. "Why are you being so difficult?" She plopped down on a chair near his desk. "I thought you loved me." Her tone was full of the exasperation she projected quite dramatically before him. Hopefully this ridiculous fit would make him see things her way. She couldn't wait when she could act like the adult she actually was. What would it take for her brother to see her that way? "Why can't you just say yes?"

"Has anyone ever told you that patience is a virtue?"

She pinned him with a ferocious glare. "Has anyone ever told you that your behavior is tedious?"

His lips twitched. "Yes," he replied in an amused tone. "You have. Several times in fact."

"It bears repeating," she said in a droll tone. "Now about the house party?"

He tapped his finger on the desk. Why wouldn't he say yes already? "All right," he conceded. "We can go. We will even leave early." He glanced at his ledgers with annoyance. They were probably why he had head pain. Calliope could sympathize. She wouldn't want that responsibility herself. "Lindsey asked me to come before his wife's family descended upon them. Have your maid pack your trunk. We will leave at dawn."

She clapped her hands in excitement. "Have I ever told you that you are my favorite brother." Thank heaven he saw reason. She couldn't wait to reach the house party and start socializing.

He narrowed his gaze. "I am your only brother."

"Then it is fortunate that I like you." She stood. "Thank you," she said in an earnest tone. "Christmas isn't your favorite time of the year. I want you to know I do understand that." She smiled. "It sounds as if the duke does too. Is that why he asked you to come early." She tilted her head to the side. "Wait... If you already planned to go, why did you tell me no?"

He shook his head. "I was going to write to Lindsey and decline the invitation. I received his missive earlier today. I haven't had time to respond." Then it was good she had come in to speak to him. He should be around people he cared about this time of the year. "Instead, I'll send it ahead of us so they know to expect our arrival."

"Oh, all right," she said absentmindedly. She had so many plans... "Then I'll let you finish your business and I'll have Lucy start packing for me. I'll see you later for the evening meal."

She left him alone in his study to go back to his ledgers. Though she did hope that he left them untouched. If he went back to work his head pain would only worsen. She preferred her brother without his grumpy side. Hopefully this Christmas he would find something good. She closed her eyes and wished happiness for her brother. If anyone needed it, he did.

***

When they finally arrived at the Lindsey estate, her brother breathed a sigh of relief—Calliope could appreciate it too. She couldn't wait to step out of the carriage and stretch her legs. When the carriage rolled to a stop at the entrance, Daniel stepped out immediately. She wished she could have as well, but it wasn't easy to exit a carriage with billowing skirts. Daniel halted long enough to assist Calliope out of the carriage. Then he stomped up the front steps and banged on the door. Damn…he was impatient.

"So kind of you to wait for me to walk with you," Calliope said as she caught up with him. "You're quite the gentleman, brother."

Daniel met her gaze and grinned. "Thank you,"

he replied in an amused tone. "I've always prided myself on being a gentleman."

Calliope rolled her eyes. "I would think most ladies consider you a scoundrel."

"Thank you," he agreed, then winked.

At that moment, the door opened. An elderly man with snow white hair and faded brown eyes stood in the entrance. "Yes?"

"I am Lord Hampstead, and this is Lady Calliope Andrews. Their Graces are expecting us." Daniel informed the older man with efficiency that Calliope could appreciate.

"Indeed," the elderly man said. "Please come in. I'll have the footman see to your trunks." He gestured for them to step into the castle.

Calliope and Daniel strolled inside. While still in the foyer, they removed their cloaks and handed them to the butler. After a few moments, the Duke of Lindsey strolled in. "Hampstead," the Duke of Lindsey said, in a jovial tone. "You're the first to arrive. I was just going to look for my wife. I trust your journey went well."

"Aside from the cold," he grumbled. "And Calliope's constant petulant complaints. Indeed, it was most pleasant." She hadn't complained that much. Calliope glared at Daniel. She had the urge to wrap her hands around his neck, but since she did love him, she refrained from murdering him.

Calliope rolled her eyes and said to the duke, "Don't listen to him, Your Grace." She smiled. "He's terrible to travel with." She would not let Daniel's attitude ruin this party for her. "We're both happy to be here. Thank you for the invitation."

The duke's lips twitched. "I'm familiar with Hampstead's dislike of travel. I understand it is a familial trait as well." His eyes gleamed with amusement. It shouldn't bother her that the duke found her dislike of travel so entertaining, but it did. "I'm glad you were both brave enough to endure it and join us. Please follow me to the sitting room. The duchess should be there with afternoon tea. Unless you would prefer to be shown to your rooms so you can rest."

"I'd prefer tea," Calliope said. She couldn't wait to become more friendly with the duchess. "I can rest later."

Daniel met the Duke of Lindsey's gaze. "I don't suppose you have brandy instead?"

Lindsey shook his head. "No, at least not in the sitting room. We can retire to my study later for a snifter or two."

"All right," Daniel agreed.

Before they could depart, another bang on the door caught their attention. The butler was nowhere to be found. Lindsey cursed and went to answer his own door. It was Daniel's turn to have an amused expression as the duke did something a servant normally would. "Goodland," the duke said in a cheery tone. "I thought you were coming later." He gestured for the viscount to come inside.

The Viscount of Goodland stepped into the foyer and unbuttoned his coat. Calliope's breath hitched at the sight of him. He was so gorgeous. Thick dark brown hair kissed by the sun. Blue eyes so deep she thought she might become lost in them. She shook those thoughts away. He might be handsome, but that didn't mean he was the man for her. She vowed to become more acquainted with him while she was there.

"I wrapped up my business early and thought, why the hell not come earlier. It won't be too much trouble, will it?" the viscount asked.

The duke of Lindsey shook his head. "No, your chamber should already be prepared. The servants have been preparing for this house party for days now."

"Wonderful," Viscount Goodland replied, and

shrugged out of his coat. The butler returned at that moment and took it from him.

"I'll take that, my lord," the butler said, then left.

The viscount turned toward Daniel and Calliope. "Hampstead," he shouted in a jovial tone. "I saw your carriage being taken to the stable. There is a stack of trunks out there to be brought inside. Did you bring your entire wardrobe with you?"

Her brother glared at him. "Only one of those trunks belongs to me."

"I'm afraid the rest are mine," Calliope said. Her cheeks pinkened as she met Goodland's gaze. "Gowns take up a lot of space."

Daniel narrowed his gaze and studied her She didn't like that look one bit. It was not a good sign. The last thing she needed was his constant supervision. "You don't need to explain yourself to the viscount. He likes to tease. Ignore him. The rest of us do." She let out a breath she'd been holding. Good he didn't think much of her response.

"He is right," the viscount agreed. "They do ignore me. Even when they shouldn't." He winked. Her heart skipped a beat. What was with her stomach. He held her hand there…why was it all aflutter? "I hope you do not follow his lead." He held a hand over his chest. "It would break what's left of my poor abused heart." Oh, she was in trouble or rather this gentleman was. He was a charmer through and through, and she was already becoming besotted with him.

"Do not listen to that nonsense," Daniel ordered Calliope. He turned to the viscount. "And you stay away from my sister."

She wanted to tell the viscount to ignore Daniel, but she held her tongue. If she hoped to become more acquainted with the viscount, then she'd have to do it in secret. What her brother didn't know wouldn't hurt him.

"Hampstead, you're being exceedingly tedious today," the viscount said in an exasperated tone.

"I think we should go for that tea now," Daniel said through gritted teeth. Oh, he really didn't like the viscount paying her any attention. She had to wonder why…

"Excellent idea," Lindsey said. "Follow me."

The duke led them down a corridor in his sprawling castle until they finally arrived at the sitting room. The duchess was indeed inside, and tea was sitting on a nearby cart. They all settled in for afternoon tea. The conversation stilted, and there was no sign that it would improve either. None of that mattered to Calliope. She had a plan, and it evolved around the Viscount of Goodland. He might not know it yet, but they were about to get very acquainted.

Order here https://books2read.com/WhenILovedaCharmer

Excerpt: Courting a Christmas Wallflower

CHRISTMAS WALLFLOWERS BOOK 12

Christmas Wallflowers
Courting a Christmas Wallflower
USA TODAY BESTSELLING AUTHOR
Dawn Brower

Prologue

Lightening flashed moments before thunder struck and rattled the windows of Evangeline Payne's bedroom. She shook beneath her blanket. Eva hated storms, but loud ones always made her nervous. This storm was no different.

Her mother, Daphne Atwood Payne, Viscountess Norwich had died during a storm like this one. That was four years earlier when Eva was three and ten. It was then when she'd become timid and lost the ability to speak well in polite company. Storms had become her greatest weakness.

Her father had changed after her mother's death too. He'd become distant and angry. His temper flared at the slightest provocation. Her stammer hadn't helped when he wanted her attention. She tried to avoid him at all costs. She relished the moments when she was allowed to visit her grandmother, Theodora, the Dowager Countess of Birchwood. At her grandmother's estate she felt free, but still even there with her three cousins for company she couldn't shake the stutter that plagued her.

She was going to stay with her grandmother in a week and she couldn't wait. The storm only made her more anxious. What if it was an omen of sorts? If her father forbade her from going Eva didn't know what she would do. She had to go. She just had to.

Eva slipped out of bed and made her way to the window. She should face her fear and maybe then she could lose the stutter too. Something had to change or she would never be able to escape her father's house. She needed to marry, and she prayed for something to help her do that.

Her hand shook as she opened the window. With it wide open wind blew inside and the rain pelted against her skin. She lifted her head and let it pour over her face. The pain that prickled her skin from the drops of water was enough to shock her to reality. This was silly. Another flash of lighting and the pound of thunder rattled around her. Eva took a deep breath and then stepped away from the window. She was tired of being afraid.

She stared at the stormy sky and made a promise to herself. This summer when she was at her grandmother's estate, she would make a change. She would become a woman a man noticed, and she would find a husband. If she couldn't do that, then she had no real chance of a future. Her father drank too much brandy and he got meaner the more foxed he became.

Eva was tired of being afraid of her own shadow. It was time to live in the light. She stepped forward and closed the windows. Storms were not going to be her weakness anymore. Instead the tempest would be her strength as she walked into the storm and faced everything it threw her way.

She slipped into bed again and settled beneath her blanket. For the first time in a long time she slept peacefully. As if fate had given her a gift. One she had been waiting for and hadn't realized it. All she had to do was accept it and her greatest desire would be hers. Finally.

One

E va stared out the window of the bedchamber she had been assigned at Seabury Castle. The castle was located along the shoreline, far outside of the village of St. Davids in Wales. It seemed almost as if her father had banished her to the ends of the earth, considering the castle's remote locale. After two failed seasons, her father had sent her to stay with her Aunt Clara, the Countess of Andover, who had found a husband in her first season. So somehow that made her the only person who could possibly help Eva find one herself.

It didn't matter to her father that Aunt Clara lived in such a remote location or that the chance Eva might meet a prospective husband would be unlikely. Eva believed her father had just wanted to send her away, and her lack of a successful season was an excuse to do so.

Aunt Clara had plenty of advice to give. Unfortunately, none of it was exceptionally useful to Eva. Her stutter made most gentlemen look upon her unfavorably, and no amount of advice Aunt Clara could give would help that particular situation.

Eva opened the blue velvet bag where she'd stored the rose quartz. Her turn had arrived to use it, and she wasn't certain she wanted to. There were certain ramifications that came with the gift the rose quartz gave that Eva didn't want to have befall her. Was finding love worth the hardships that may happen as a result? Hadn't she already endured enough. Why did love have to be difficult, too?

Carefully, Eva placed the rose quartz back inside the velvet bag and pulled the strings to close it tight, then put the bag inside the drawer on her writing desk. It would be safe there. She refused to place the necklace around her neck. Eva was afraid to invoke the supposed magical properties it contained. She wanted freedom from her current circumstances, but at what cost? What would the rose quartz expect of her in return for granting her a chance with her one true love?

No, she couldn't do it. Even if it meant she would never find love… She would not risk something happening to the one person meant for her. Fate was fickle, and she would not tempt it to a disastrous end. She would take her chances with whatever her lot in life turned out to be without the aid of the rose quartz. After a time, she'd send it on to her cousin, the final one of four of them, to allow her a turn. She had to at least pretend she was interested in the rose quartz for now. Eva didn't wish to give her cousins a reason to question her or her motives. They all seemed fine with using the quartz to find love, and if she expressed any disinterest, she feared how they might react. This was what was best for her, and she didn't want to explain herself to anyone.

A knock echoed through the chamber, causing Eva to jump. She turned toward the door. Who could be on the other side? She prayed it wasn't her aunt. Eva had been in residence at the castle for less than a sennight and already her aunt was driving her mad. Another knock. "Miss Payne," a woman said from the other side of the door. "Lady Andover wishes for you to join her in the blue salon."

Eva groaned. She was probably preparing more lessons for Eva. So far none of her lessons had made much sense. Truthfully, they were nothing more than her aunt regaling her with tales of her own season and the joys of her youth. Eva had been polite, of course, but she had been battling ennui the entire time. "Please tell her I'll join her posthaste." She kept her tone light and happy sounding and somehow managed not to stutter once. Eva did not need the maid to report her lack of enthusiasm to Aunt Clara.

She sighed and then took a deep, fortifying breath. When she faced her aunt, she would need whatever strength she could muster. Satisfied she was duly prepared for the upcoming encounter with her aunt, she smoothed her skirts one last time, then exited her chamber. Eva slowly descended the stairs. Ladies, as her aunt had said often since she'd arrived, did not run or rush to be anywhere. It would be foolish to start the encounter with a lecture on her hurried arrival.

Once she stepped inside the parlor, she waited by the entrance for her aunt to acknowledge her. Aunt Clara had a fair complexion not marred by any time spent outdoor. Her hair was dark, almost as dark as the night sky, but highlighted slightly by some silver streaked throughout. When she turned toward Eva, her blue eyes made her shiver slightly from the coldness of their depths.

"Evangeline," her aunt greeted her. "Come forward, girl, and sit. I don't want to look up at you the entire time."

Eva swallowed the lump in her throat and did as her aunt asked. She sat in the chair directly across from her aunt. When she had first arrived, she had deigned to sit closer and come to regret that decision. It was far easier for her aunt to reach out and smack her with her cane if she was within reach. "The maid told me you required me to attend to you." Eva struggled not to stutter. She was afraid of Aunt Clara, but if she couldn't keep from stumbling over the words, her aunt would find some way to punish her for it. The few days she'd spent in her company had been harsh ones, and forced her to speak very carefully. She never let words spill off her tongue without first thinking about what she should say and then deliberately pronouncing each one.

"Yes," her aunt agreed. "I did send for you. There are a few things we need to discuss."

That did not bode well for Eva... "About?" She lifted a brow. Eva probably should refrain from being impertinent, but this was something she had to know.

"Your future, of course," her aunt clarified. "I see no reason why you have not secured a match yet. You come from a solid family line and you are passably pretty."

Such kind words her aunt had for her... Eva barely managed to suppress the urge to roll her eyes. Besides, her aunt was right. She did come from an excellent family and her blonde hair and blue eyes were at least more favorable in the eyes of the ton. Those things had never been the issue. She glanced away from her aunt and tried to keep the fear from her voice, but failed. "It..s not my fam... fam...family connections." Damn it. She'd been doing so well.

"No," her aunt agreed. The disapproval in her tone was evident as she spoke. "But we can work on your...speech difficulties."

Eva turned to face her aunt. "I've bbbeen trying," she said. Shame spread through her as she spoke. Why couldn't she stop stuttering?

"Not hard enough," Aunt Clara said in a firm tone. "But we are going to ensure that will no longer be a deterrent for you. Starting with a house party over Christmastide."

She forced herself to calm down and articulate her words. Eva had to keep her wits about her to navigate the rest of their conversation, and stuttering would make it all inherently worse. "A house party?" She thought she would be free from social engagements until the start of the season. That had been the only blessing she could see about being sent to the remote area of Wales. "Christmastide is a mere sennight away. Is there time to arrange it?"

"I have already begun doing so." Her aunt leaned forward, pressing her cane into the carpet. "Invitations were sent before you arrived. Our first guests will start to arrive tomorrow."

How awful… Why was her aunt just now telling her this? There was no helping any of it of course. This was her life for the foreseeable future. Her aunt had complete control over her. Eva's father had ensured that when he'd exiled her to the castle. "How many guests will be here?"

"Several gentlemen," her aunt informed her. "At least three eligible ones. I had to invite some ladies too or it wouldn't be even numbers in attendance, and well, it would not look right. If I were you, I'd take advantage of the close proximity and lure one of those gentlemen into matrimony."

Surely her aunt wasn't suggesting she trap one

of them into marriage. That couldn't be right at all. Aunt Clara was far too prudish to suggest anything so untoward. "I don't know if that is possible, but I will try to gain the attention of one of them."

"Do more than that." Her aunt's tone was firm. "I expect that after Christmastide, I can write your father of your impending nuptials." She stared at Eva for several moments, unblinking. "Do not let me down, girl."

What else was she supposed to say to that? She would not trap some unsuspecting gentleman into marriage. Eva wanted more than that with a husband. She hoped to find love, or at the very least, a mutual respect. If she forced a man to marry her, surely he would come to resent her for it. "I promise to do my best." She would not promise to do anything she found appalling.

"That's what I'm afraid of." Her aunt sighed. "But don't you worry, girl, I'm here, and I will not allow you to fail."

And that was what Eva feared after hearing what her aunt had to say. If Eva couldn't force a marriage to happen, her aunt would. This upcoming house party would be a social disaster. If she didn't find a husband, she might very well end up ruined at the end of it.

"I'm certain that will make my father happy." Eva didn't believe her father cared what happened to her as long as he was no longer responsible for her care. She was not a male child and therefore he had little use for her. He'd married not long ago and was doing his best to impregnate his new bride with his heir. Eva was not important.

"Of course he will be. That is why he sent you to me, after all." Aunt Clara lifted her chin. There was a smugness in her gaze that was foreboding. "I have also had the maids go through your gowns. Most will be fine for the house party but you did not bring any ballgowns. A seamstress will be here in the morning to take your measurements. You will be dressed appropriately for the Christmas ball. That is when I hope to announce your betrothal."

Her aunt was overconfident about her chances of securing a match at this house party. What would she do when Eva undoubtedly failed? She wanted to run and hide, but that would not solve her problem. It was time to put her head high and quit being the timid mouse she'd been for years. "All right," she said in a soft tone. "Is there anything else?" She hoped not…

"No," Aunt Clara said. "Go rest. It will be the last time you can for a while. Tomorrow is the start of your new future. Prepare yourself, because nothing will ever be the same again."

Eva nodded. "Yes, Aunt Clara," she said, then turned on her heels to leave. She didn't have to wait until the next day for her life to change. It had the moment she'd been told she would have to stay in Wales over the winter months. Nothing had been the same since her father had decreed his sister would be her tutor and help Eva find a husband. She had known then that her life would be full of constant upheaval, and the fact she'd been right did not make it better. She walked slowly to her chamber, and once there plopped down on the bed and gave in to the urge to cry. Later, there would be no time for tears, and it was best to get the anguish out and only show strength afterward. If she had any chance of helping herself, she would have to find her inner strength and hold on to it with all she had inside of her. She couldn't counsel herself. All she could do was try to be reasonable and move forward as best she could.

Order Here: https:// books2read.com/CourtingWallflower